Vampire Count

HIDDEN DRAGON

Steve H Hakes

Vampire Count

Hidden Dragon

Steve H Hakes

Paperback ISBN: 978-1-8380946-1-4

Hardback ISBN: 979-8-4483293-9-5

Kindle ISBN: 978-1-8380946-0-7

V250813103758:   simbolinian@outlook.com

Thanks to...

- Sheridan Le Fanu's non-lesbian, *Carmilla* (1872)
- Christian songwriter/vampire writer, Sabine Baring-Gould's, *Margery of Quether* (1891)
- Bram Stoker's folk-Catholic, *Dracula* (1897)

Was this the end? Was death bittersweet? As the sun set he looked back on his life. The days had often been dark; his home had long perished into oblivion. Simboliniad the crystal planet, was no more, mercilessly crushed by the Milky Way, its dust probably just scattered around the Monoceros Ring. Like moths having lost their light, its race of Pneumata had migrated *en masse* through deep heaven, until eventually their hearts were strangely warmed towards the early forming of a blue marble planet, the third planet in the Field of Arbol, Arda, which seemed somehow to beckon them in.

Alas, they had seen and returned its greetings from afar, and approaching closely had only done so on the presumption that they were but strangers and aliens, soon to depart to they knew not where. Theirs was to wonder, then to wander, but in coming too close it was as if planetary tentacles had embraced them with a love that would not let them go. A fish might lament the loving embrace of an octopus, but at least it is fair game, but a flower that captures a bee, simply isn't playing the game.

Soon their affection for this planet paled, and the wonder of birth gave way to the shackling of spirits, spirits in bondage, spirits resentful, spirits rebellious. For the planet maker, Usen himself, had set a special law that prohibited Pneumata from leaving this new world, if by their own free will they had entered its orb. That law they had neither known nor bargained for. Admittedly, it was not as if they found this world—happily within the Goldilocks zone—to be without great enchantment. Indeed to hang around as it slowly formed, had at first seemed a tremendous joy and privilege for spectators to the unfolding game of life. But they were also free spirits, so resentment easily set in, once they discovered that they had become shackled into this world's history without escape, even as much much later mariners would get sucked inescapably into Charybdis—though for the latter their world history would end swiftly within that watery grave. More blessèd were they!

Till death you do part? It was a bit like a marriage. Bound for life, you must like it or lump it, but you have made your bed. Well not quite like, for marriage can be disloyally opted out from, betrayed, whereas by strictly enforcing the Eighth Law, the Powers kept the Pneumata *per force* from leaving, and unlike marriage they had never consented. It was more like what some would call a forced marriage—or in fact, forced slavery. Though knowledge of Usen was universal, some creatures undoubtedly knew him better than others. Kindly souls defined him as goodness which did good. That sounded very clever, but less flattering definitions existed.

Do you really wish to know? Well, the Simbolinians seemed to be getting to know him and his ways all too well. Yes, he was greatness itself, the source of all, and it was glaringly obvious that his works were great. But one can be both great and bad. Put it this way, this world would, by and by, birth a biozone. Wow, few worlds could match that! Yet that biozone would include vegetation that produced a deceptively sweet plant, one which insects would love to visit to their doom, honeytraps to swallow the gullible.

Likewise love—which later on Usen's secondborn would sometimes express as Venus (one of their names for a neighbouring planet)—could be sweet but deadly, both a lovely flower and a trap for flies. Analogically, did this not *inter alia* illustrate Usen as the cosmic trap-maker? Were not the Simbolinians as flies being absorbed into this new world, as insects fatally trapped within a perfumed and flowery pit of corruption? Talk of fatal attraction! Had they been evil? No. Well, maybe. It was difficult to judge. It certainly was true that after the entrapment, most turned to evil, to the Dark Side, to creatures conceived beyond time and space, Powers which had for other reasons rebelled against Usen. But what should Usen have expected? He kicked them; they kicked back, reason against unreason.

More about Usen, would you know? Well, he was certainly controversial, so that how he was described depended on who you asked. Fair doos, he sometimes united—but only on his terms. More disturbingly he divided, and shamelessly made no bones about it. He even divided Simbolinian from Simbolinian. He said that he only divided to offer the ultimate unity.

Well, the few who swallowed that, were swiftly accounted fools by the many, but they held back from rebellion. Exactly why they really held back, wasn't clear to the others. Was it fear of judgement? All knew that Usen held the cosmic stick. Was it simple stupidity? Did they think that he held a cosmic carrot?

Little by little, those of the Light grew further apart from those of the Night, from the realists of the real world. In fact the epitaph, night, for long remained an ethical descriptor only. This planet spun around, generating gravity, and in turn kept itself rotating around its star and its axis. Whatever they thought about Usen, none had any problem with moving around in the light of day, or in the darkness of night. And of those nights and days—together called days—they lost count. In fact they never really bothered to count mere days. Nor journeys around the star, what some would call years. They sensed time in the billions of years. Many planets were birthed and died before the Simbolinians even noticed that sunshine was becoming a problem for their physical eyes.

One clear indicator of that problem began with the dimming of Arda. This phenomenon began before, and went into, the Philikoi Years. A mysterious planetwide shroud of mist-enveloping darkness developed, and only specks of sunlight and starlight managed to seep through. The silvery moon? Forget it! Terrestrial life suffered terribly, but by feeling some short-term relief, the vampires of the Night realised that sunshine had become less friendly to them. *Don't let the morning come, bringing the sun, I just want to live on in the night.* When the Philikoi took over management, they comprehended not the shroud, and were at a loss. Then, to give light, they created global lamps of blue and gold, yet they came to nought by evil undoing.

Then they made luminous trees of silver and gold, yet the trees were killed. Yet by the dying trees, they managed to kick-start the sunshine, and again there was moonshine as the shroud was burnt away, and Necuratu retreated into his own darkness. Strange it was that in killing the trees, the spider source of the sky shroud had been revealed, and that the poison of death proved to be the very antidote to heal the sickly skies: if death kills death, the shortterm victory of Hadēs is but hollow. For the Philikoi revealed the glories of moon and sun, and sailing though Arda's orb they healed the skies. It is prophesied that when the secondborn put on immortality, then these high level Guardians of sun and moon, will return to the Deathless

City, which will then have no need of sun or moon, for it will have the imperishable light of Kabod.

Unlike the Night, vampires of the Dawn grieved the sun's dimming, as of a friend's death. This toleration by the light, contrasting with intolerance by the Night, exacerbated resentment by those of the Night. The two sides had long crystallised into two kingdoms, the Dawn and the Night, but they had never fallen into civil war—why is war never un-civil? But they had long acclimatised to assassinations both sides of the ideological border, usually by the Night, but then numbers were on the side of the Night Kingdom. In fact, by this time, both sides had made a more or less tacit agreement to stick to their own sides of daytime and nighttime hours. For less contact, meant less confrontation between the sides.

A shame to fall out, really, but the rifts radically widened and deepened once the Children of Usen came into the equation. For long this new world had been mineral only. Then Usen had blessed—or cursed it, depending on perspective—with biology, intelligent self-replicating code: an island doesn't cry; its creatures certainly do. Yes, cells were created intelligent, but at first produced no intelligence, no brains, no CPUs to coordinate bodies, no personhood arising from higher brains, not even personality. Vegetation had formed along established lines of DNA coding. Such life was so simple.

Then biological life had extended to animal life, and there arose peoples of brain, both personality and personhood, *hnau*, endowed with the special blessing of the Guardians. Animal life had joined the spiritual dimension. These peoples could know beyond themselves, beyond the universe, could tap into logic, deduce what must be around the corner, comprehend laws that governed nature. They could know Usen, and children of his they were.

Biological evolution was never random, but was created with inbuilt intelligent self-programming, able to unfold itself into new species and types, and was indeed a marvellous process to behold. But sadly it further separated the Simbolinians. Perhaps it boiled down to blood, the haves, and the have nots. Once upon a time, Simbolinians simply feasted on cosmic rays—perhaps sunshine had been more needed than those who now despised it had realised. Once, they had been creatures of will without physical bodies, thelosomatic spirits.

But entrapped on this planet, they had slowly adapted to absorb what they slowly needed to need.

Through psychic, one might even say spiritual process, they began to extract life for the physical bodies that they had enrobed themselves with, as they had slowly come to fit in with this world—the process of integration. By default that body shape was now humanoid, copied from the Children, yet significantly modified, and within that shape they could relax and roam the material world. But being primarily creatures of will, they remained shapeshifters, and could morph their humanoid shapes into other shapes at will, and had done so in earlier times. In the gigayears of their first strength, that had been easy enough, but in later ages the going had become tougher. The very weak had even struggled to keep body and soul together in humanoid mode, let alone going in for fancy shapeshifting stunts.

Sure, even before the arrival of the Children, the Simbolinians had developed a need to eat, or rather to absorb, physical nourishment. The simple fact was that to create a DNA shell—and they had first favoured the bat and the wolf—created a shell of needs. Maybe creating weakness had been a big mistake, but they had soon found that they could emulate the eating that they saw evolving in the animal kingdom, transmuting flesh and muscle into bodily sustenance, changing its matrix. Soon they had realised that one mortal element in particular could be ideally transmuted by their will power—by their thelodynamics—into their physical form. That element was...blood. Why munch, when drinking is far richer and easier for the needs of the body? That's when they had become vampires, blood drinkers.

And the bust up? Well, although not until the tree-years were all but ended, the Kingdom of Night discovered that the Children of Usen were an ideal source of blood, although the idea troubled King Elaran, for he feared comeback. But some soon argued that by attacking the Children they justifiably attacked the Father. The loudest naysayers were the Simbolinians of Dawn. Though they had become vampires, bloodsuckers, they deemed that drinking the blood of the Children was a serious sacrilege. Thou shalt have, or thou shalt not have? That was the question of blood. Thus both sides confronted each other, and fights broke out, eventually forming into more assassinations, vampire against vampire. But always by stealth, and only if a vampire really was annoying in seeking to dine or to deliver. Neither kingdom fancied the idea of all-out war. The king forbade any blood fest, partly to diffuse tension between those of the Night and those of the Dawn—why up the ante? But by withholding his side from wholesome blood, they became less likely to withhold their hands against him—politically inexpedient, his days were numbered.

Thus it was that in the sun-year of 1.60, voices were raised within the Night Kingdom, voices of power, voices seeking control. One of the mighty arose. Having long pondered in his heart the force of fear, he conceived in his mind a mighty shape of fear. He transformed himself into a gigantic snake—or one might say lizard, for it had legs. But to this shape he combined the webbed wings of a mighty bat. From a flier of skies long fallen, he formed a somewhat tapered teeth-strewn beak, yet hooked and stubbier. From the insect world, he had studied a beetle which could eject a caustic chemical from behind as it fled.

But soaring fight, not fleeing flight, burned in the heart of this vampire lord. He was a confronter, and from his mouth he came to spew fire, as if spewed from the very volcanoes of deepest perdition. Fire and smoke, from a burning heart of fire, which consumed but was not consumed, for he could create fire from his inmost being, juggling atoms at will. He became a shape of terror, an impressive figure from which to launch his leadership bid—if ever that day should come. This shape the Lord of Necros envied, and soon copied the idea through his own dark arts. And thus into the world would begin the days of the dragons, to which pterosaurs had been but a sideshow, an adumbration.

The true inventor was soon rebranded *Angruin*, Iron Fire—and he was not displeased. Yet he created this form to frighten, not to fight, the Children. Towards them he had no cause to fight, yet as toys he played with their fears and their flight—a few killings added zest to the game, rounded off with a good pint. For all his razzmatazz, he was not one iota stronger when gallivanting around in his dragon shape, but it puffed up his vanity and could daunt many who judged by outward appearances. Even as nature can mark the venomous, his shape showed his inner poison. Vampire *weltschmerz* was stirring among the community, due to the craven king's contumacy, and

Angruin foresaw that his mastery of masks might well bode well for any new election, especially if backed by the Turannoi. The Powers had basic skills in shapes, but the Pneumata had developed these skills, and among them Angruin had become the master, working long on rearranging DNA code through matings with animal kind—he disposed of offspring quickly and quietly, even as an artist bins their experimental sketches: he did not need them.

The dragon shape was his latest and greatest design, too good to keep secret. Soon he was boasting away to Necuratu, to whom—almost from Day One—he had gravitated towards as a kindred spirit. Within his own dark designs, the Dark Lord weighed up this fearsome mask. As a Power, of course he had the basics of shapeshifting, and could adapt it to warfare. But must he wage war from the front?

In his war with the firstborn, the Dark Lord now conceived the idea of creating a whole race of fire-breathers, always at his beck and call—but a mere vampire must not get the credit! Moreover, he needed more servants more than a new shape for himself, servants that could only multiply by biology. To merely copy the art of Angruin, would be to play second fiddle. But Necuratu would only be first. In his heart he hated all rivals to his power, but his power had waned. Under the Cosmic King, the Kingdom Powers of the deathless land had clipped his wings, and ignominiously kept him in check through mere Psuchai. The Children had him boxed in within his own fortress, he, who would be master of the universe!

Necuratu felt bitter. He had been put down by the Philikoi, but was he not greater than any of them, greater even than the Elder King—their king under Usen? Yes, but that greatness was because he had a good dollop of all of their specialist skills. Thus, while unable to beat any level-one Power at their own speciality, the sheer breadth of his skill base was more than enough to pose a threat to several of them together. He was a jack of all trades, though master of none. Correction, he was a master of control, and had many second-level Powers at his call, Powers which had fallen along with him under the banner *Non Serviem*.

Strange how they, refusing to serve Usen the Source, were forced to serve Necuratu the Derivative. They discovered too late that the rebellion had enslaved them from freedom and to despair. They were in their right mind, but their goose was cooked; they had made their bed and had to lie on it eternally, though it be a bed of ice-cold gold.

Even in their most diabolical broodings, none neither desired nor dared to dream of repenting, surrendering, although a few might make some semblance of half-hearted repentance under pressure, as the line of least resistance. No, their only safety from Usen lay in supporting Necuratu, with whom they shared the same hate of the imperishable light. Otherwise they would be a divided kingdom, killed on collapse.

For Powers, being killed meant not the death of the body—they had no inherent biology—but meant being thrust through the Door of Night into the Timeless Void, a dimension of pure unadulterated individualism, continuity without community, meaningless ghosthood in which language, and therefore thought, was lost. Pride kept them together; pride kept them apart. Necuratu was not going to play second fiddle to a Pneuma, so when the boastful Angruin left, the Dark Lord summoned a favourite slave into his unlit labyrinth, and propounded his plan unto her.

"Urnúla, behold how Angruin robes himself in his pride. Just like us he loves not Usen's children, yet unlike us he hates them not. The fool is content for them to bow before him in fear, rather than to crush them. Yet thou art a spirit of fire and of mystery, and for thee I have devised a new way to serve me. Hearken, thou must don flesh as of a beast that creepest over the earth. As one with them thou must mate with them, thus with the skill stolen from Angruin, conceiving in thy being reptiles that will grow into monstrous size and strength, with heat within that canst melt the strongest of swords. Then they shall mate among themselves, male and female, producing after their kind in defiance of Usen. For his children trouble my kingdom, and my servants of flesh are no match for the firstborn.

"Yet I, if I break forth in naked power, would be assailed by the Powers of the West. Strong allies shall I need against that day. And through thee a new power can be unleashed, yet not winged, lest the great eagles should challenge them. Nor would I have them too alike to Angruin the Arrogant, lest he mock me. Yet Usen's children shall wither before my fire-worms." Thus spake Necuratu, and it was so, for Urnúla was to him a slave, not a counsellor, and she knew it well, and she had skills of fire.

Usen could be abhorred, but he could not be avoided, and abhorrent predictions of doom sometimes were spoken into the Kingdom of Necros—or of Night. Urnúla, trembling before her dark lord, looked up, a strange light in her eyes. With a voice not her own, as a seer she spoke dire warning. "Necuratu of many names of darkness and of folly, consider The One you cannot avoid. Think not that you must climb into the deep heavens to find him, for even if you lay low in the world of death he will be there, as light inescapable which sees the very thoughts of your dark heart. You have fled from him to this world, and he has hemmed you in, defeated rebel who would defeat all. Unjustly you have sought to spoil his ways. Much hurt and harm have you done, yet there is healing and rebirth beyond the reach of your poison and your power.

"Woe to you. You shall be cast out shapeless beyond the Walls of Night, though the sickness of your will will long blight this world and seek its choice. And close confined will you stay, witless and powerless, even nigh until the End of Days, and others shall embody evil within creation, to its despite. Yet creation will watch and see that evil ever consumes itself, and those of the Light shall be the wiser and more glorious.

"From Angruin, you have in secrecy seen new shapes, and your heart is swollen in pride. Since urulóki you shall release, as a dragon you yourself shall descend as days' end. For you yourself will be released for a short space, even if for a millennium, to rebuild in that season your kingdom, for you yourself shall see the fullness of justice before your final fate. For a final sword awaits you, you who are always apt to slay. Hater of grace and justice, they will come for you through the herald of glad tidings.

"Of his name, who can fully know? To the end of your kingdom, he shall ride to war in sovereign power upon a white horse; his eyes will be as flames of fire; his robe shall be a battle dress dyed in the blood of his enemies. Then shall your people exclaim, *Alas, how the mighty has fallen.*" With words of doom ended the voice not of Urnúla, as spent she sank down before her lord, and her eyes became black. His heart trembled, yet his mind resolved to do as much harm as he could, before facing the wrath of Usen—for his heart was black. Dragons would make the world tremble before him.

No *de novo* creation was needed, simply creative code changes in genetic makeup, piggybacking on the very coding given by Usen and conceived in goodness, changes coupled with the evil will of the Turannoi. So, inspired by Angruin, ordered by Necuratu, and developed by Urnúla, diaboloi-controlled monsters were soon raised and let loose upon the earth. But Urnúla, mother of the first wingless drakes, would soon be forgotten in the macrohistory of Middle-earth. She was but the mother by her master's will. And Angruin? He was but the inventor of the shape, the inventor whom proud Necuratu preferred to forget. And Necuratu was a revisionist, a deceiver. Credit given where credit is due, is a saw not always honoured among thieves, but being unaccredited with the basic design of the new creatures, galled the pride of Angruin.

But walls have ears, especially for a telepath, and all too soon he had heard that the Dark Lord had thanklessly ripped off his idea and gone into production. He himself had considered urging his people to be at one with the Necros, for which he had strong affinity. Though he was of evil desire and darkened mind, pride now prohibited promoting Necuratu who had cheated him. Had he come to dominate his people, it might be that he would otherwise have steered them into the Necrotic Kingdom, and a greater evil would have arisen.

As it was, he knew better than to challenge the first dragon of Necuratu, for a direct challenge to his kingdom would lead to a war which neither desired—if evil fights evil, evil must lose. And the slain would face damnation the sooner. So the only good that came out of Necuratu's pride, was that Angruin would for that time terminate his willing cooperation with the Necros, in muted protest, ironically playing into the hands of the Kingdom of Light.

Two

ℰNTER THE DRAGON

Angruin was all alone. Alone, depression could easily have set in, yet anger soon moved in for company. Yes, he and his anger would survive and would wreak havoc. There was no love lost between he and his father, nor he and his brother, but then love was despised and rejected in the Kingdom of Night. There was respect, respect of power. And there was fear, a road to power, to dominance. Already he was a prince, adopted for his skills to a seat at the king's left hand. And he was the first dragon, the blueprint of a race that would soon arise, yet as blueprint he would soon be forgotten. Still, his pride was justifiably great. The slow rise and fall of the dragon race was yet to be; the Dark Lord was ever slow.

If not for wounded pride, Angruin of the vampires, and not Urnúla of the diaboloi, might have been the progenitor of the race of dragons. But offended beyond words, he had henceforth discarded the Kingdom of Necros, and geared up his mind to build up his own kingdom. He could not but envy Necuratu the Thief's plan: a race of lesser creatures could possibly dominate the Children of Usen.

But he swiftly realised that if he now created his own dragon host, or even tried to get in first, then war between him and proud Necuratu would ensue, and going head to head, as Night against Necros, was unwise: pride can be the first step to destruction. Nevertheless, within his heart he vaguely toyed with an idea of somewhere down the line, devising a race of giants, perhaps by mating his people with Usen's children. But for now, he must be content to range far and free in his new shape, causing consternation among the Children for kicks and for kudos. His anger at the one party, triggered anger towards the other. Man kicks woman; woman kicks dog.

Hidden away within the Blue Mountains, Gimrulim of the Firebeards first saw the winged menace in the water soaked skies. "To arms," he cried, "'ware the skies", shaking his axe in token of challenge. Nekket too grabbed axe, brandishing it towards the unknown creature. Fools they were, but fearless fools. At their cry, many more dwarves blazed forth from their mansion, what some merely called mines. Perceiving as he circled, these ungainly caricatures of the Children, these adoptees, Angruin turned his first fury upon them. Fire belched from his mouth, and along with half a dozen more, neither Gimrulim nor Nekket ever again delved deeply in Middle-earth. This was warfare totally new and unstoppable, for from fire the dwarves had not yet built any defence. What were axes against airborne attack? Nevertheless, dwarves were little given to running from battle.

The dragon swooped low and fried another dozen before landing. Thokorlum rallied his fellows, and together they swarmed against Angruin. He wished to test whether their weapons would pierce his armour. If so, he could engage a thelodynamic shield of power, besides healing any harm done. "Die!" bellowed Thokorlum, and die he did. Dwaer was luckier. His axe seared through the scales of his foe, but a swipe of its tail felled him before the gates.

Angruin felt the pain, and reinforced his shape. He made a mental note to add strength to his scales, but for now he must be content to lick his wounds, for having dispatched the dwarves at the gates, Tunli was withdrawing his companions from the battle. "Back," he cried, "back from the gate. Our enemy cannot enter, our gate is too small. Back. We must outmaster this foe with cunning, with armour that will resist fire. Our revenge will come, but not if we now perish. Back!" And so it was that the first dragon attack was endured by the Cave Kingdom, and resentment would be harboured deep within the hearts of the dwarves of the mountain.

∞

Many years had come and gone. Though it was before the Long Peace, yet all was calm and the sun shone. The Dark Enemy had been hemmed in, though raiding parties, slipping through the net, remained a threat to the free peoples. Silgossel and Caliglin were perched high up in the trees, their forest protected by the Power wedded to their king. She it was who stood between that kingdom and the increasingly hostile world.

They still hoped for peace, to live and let live, yet like a cancer of evil the Enemy, currently in remission, had someday to be fought. Some suspected that his aim was not even to have a Necrotic Kingdom of slaves, but to bleed dry such slaves until biology was buried, without even trace of vegetation, a world of wraiths needing not nature. In later times, dragons could be content to rest on their beds of geneless gems, content in the knowledge that they had stolen, killed, and destroyed. But they would still need to eat; the Dark Lord would not. He sought to be master of the Doom of Arda; master of Desolation. With such a foe, peace at best was a lull in hostilities, putting off a grievous day, perhaps their final day in Middle-earth. For them the seasons came as waves breaking upon the shore, and the mortal years of the secondborn were but as ripples upon an incoming tide.

It was indeed a feature of their fair race, that a feast to the eyes was a feast to their souls, helping sustain their physical bodies. And so in joy they sat and feasted, taking in beauty and being enriched in its abundance. "Caliglin, my love, behold how beautiful the trees are in this sweet season. Would that we could sit forever here on sunlit and starlit dome. And yet the Black Lord would ravage the land, wantonly hew the trees and poison their very roots. Alas for the evil will of the Turannoi, but joy we have for a little time at least, in peace from the outside world."

"That is true beloved, and by her enchantments may our queen long protect us from our enemies. Some would that I counselled ignoble ease and peaceful sloth. I grieve that we do little more than remain within our shrunken kingdom. I grieve that beyond our fence, so much in Arda has been scarred by the Dark Hand, starved of beauty.

"Yet our queen's power is more for defence than offence, and our king will not fight alongside those who slew their kin, forbidding even their language. Yet what would our united force accomplish against such a foe, the greatest of the Great Powers, if the Powers themselves come not forth against him? And would their intervention that not unmake Middle-earth, which now is but marred? Yet Silgossel, we must bide our time, until new counsels arise, and new force comes unlooked for to our aid. But still the swift passing of years is sweet to me, while you are by my side."

With eyes of love he looked at her, seeing into her heart. And in their love they both looked unto the music of the trees, as the wind gently stirred them to their speech of yearning. Truly the wild wood was wonderful to those with the woodcraft to see and hear. The Sindeldi now sought to understand, not to tame, the wood—to tap into its very heart and soul. Such oneness was still fresh to them, for in part it was due to their guests, the Laegrim, who had fostered in them a true love of the woods. That love that desired the woods to flourish, even if they themselves perished—appreciative love. They sat in silence as the sun set, and the sun rose, set again, and beckoned to rise again. Still they sat in silence, breathing in the life of the forest.

A deep mist rolled in from the moonlit sea, and soon the ocean of trees had become an ocean of mist. As it rose, the two were enveloped by an ethereal haze silencing the silvery sheen of moonlight. Caliglin stirred. "How strange my love, that though you are beside me, you are veiled from my sight. Does the physical speak true of the metaphysical, or is the physical an imperfect shadow of the metaphysical, prophesying only in part? Surely the beauty that we see, the veil of endless beauty be. Has not Eru foretold that, though within the circles of the world, one day we shall go beyond the enshrouding mists of Middle-earth, even unto Aman? There we shall never be helplessly unhappy, as in these dying lands."

"Truly", spoke the voice of Silgossel, "in the dawning of the morning of that bright and happy day, we shall know each other better—when the mists have rolled away. Then in the deathless lands we may see all as they really are, and love all of the Light without favour or fear. In this world, it can seem that we walk alone, yet we need not walk in despair. Treachery we have tasted, yet treachery also troubles the Dark Lord. For have not even the orchoth shown that they are not safe from the Light?"

Her people knew little of that race, save that it was malevolent. Their origin was uncertain. Had rogue kwendî attacked the dwellers of Gundabad? If so, had they then murdered the wives, and taken to wife the maids? If so, had the mockery of Ibauglir brought forth an accursed offspring, an abominable mix of both the Adopted and the Children, who soon formed their own dwellings and multiplied, male and female after the manner of the Children—but of lesser mortal years? That would explain why, like dwarf women, their maidens were fewer and seldom came forth. Had—as offspring of unhappy marriages, as outcasts from both mothers and fathers—they become adoptees of the Enemy? Had he twisted them in deformity and deception, ensuring their enduring enmity with the free peoples? If these ifs spoke true of their origins, was it one of the greatest sins of the Dark Enemy?

The Sindeldi had believed that an orch could as easily become benevolent, as a leopard could change its spots, but had of late witnessed such change. "Yes, hope most wondrous. Never did we believe that friendship could exist among that woebegotten race, ever open to the beck and call of their Dark Master, yet two, named Curbag and Vitgurat, have handed themselves over to us, and brought us a mighty gift, too. The Enemy seeks to devour the very waters of life that flow through this land, but hope springs eternal. He may win for a season, but not all goes his way", said Caliglin, having recently come from the king's judgement.

∞

Standing before the king had stood two orchoth, surrounded by many guards, their captain holding a grim sword. The king gazed at his gathered people. "Truly wonders never cease. For here stand Curbag and Vitgurat, orchoth who claim to have deserted both their kind and their master. They have cast themselves upon our mercy. Yet in these perilous days, it would be unwise to take their words without judgement. O miserable orchoth of a miserable race, why stand ye here before your enemies, and what know ye of mercy?" the king had sternly demanded.

"I am Vitgurat, O king. You speak of mercy. We were ordered to raid the dwarves, flush 'em out of their caves. Gar, what choice did we have? The Big Lord would freeze our blood and flay our skins alive, as soon as look at us. You don't give him no lip, or he'll cut it off quick smart. Of course we went, and of course we fought. Yet Curbag and I alone found their forge, and their old mastersmith there alone with a sentient sword of his youth—or so he said. But he was dying, bleeding badly, could hardly lift it yet alone wield it, since some of our lads had got at him first. What a sword, not that we could have kept it, nar, higher ups always take what they can from orchoth.

"And we don't dare try to hide owt—never know who's a trusty lad and who ain't. But Curbag and me, well, growing up together we've looked out for each other. Never known why, for that's rare among us, when most just cover their own hide. And we've gotten sick of slaughter—in the early days it was fun, but why should redbeards always be enemies, anyway? Can't some be like us? And if so then why kill 'em? Nah, we don't like taking orders no more."

"Right", said Curbag. "My idea: kill smith, hide sword. All quiet? Go back. Smith wanted out. Fine, that's mercy, eh? Told him, stand still, sort you quick an' easy—no muckin', no messin'. Boss gets head, pleased as punch. Head on pikestaff, his. Sword, yours. Only one owner. Called

Troll-killer. Troll blood fresh on. Sword like that, help you fight, eh? Leave us be. Don't blab. We scarper. Hide deep from Big Boss."

"How shall we know that you are not spies, infiltrating under cloak of benevolence and baksheesh? Never have orchoth proved true. And why should we risk war with the dwarves, if ye be under our shield, and they should seek your blood in revenge?" enquired the king.

"So wise, eh? We give sword. King stab in back! Throw to dwarf mattocks, eh? Curse you! What price mercy?" Curbag was livid. Seldom had he sought to do good, to help someone else out. Do evil and you're in good company. Do good and you're in evil company. "Didn't do no harm. Didn't deceive, no. Just want leave alone. Sort ourselves. Go away from war. Don't trust bloody-handed Sindeldi, eh? Bad as Big Boss! Bah!"

"Peace," said the king, "lest folly become your undoing, if you liken us to the Dark Lord. For you have said that he would not spend time looking on you, yet alone in speaking with you. Yet unlike him I look and must ask, if I am to spare you. Again I ask: how can I be sure that you are not a trap set for my feet, baseborn bringers of woe?"

Vitgurat it was who answered. "O king, forgive Curbag's anger—he spoke as an accursed fool. If you fear us, send us to where we can't see what you're up to, and can't tell no one no how. Would you kill a fangless snake? And if the foulbeards find us, then let 'em come and get us and they'll weep in payment of our deaths. No skin off your nose. Just don't blab that we're here."

"That you defend Curbag to me, speaks to me of kindliness beyond your kind, strange though I find that in an orch. Such thoughts as were in my mind, you have spoken, and spoken well, or so I judge. For it was to test you that I spoke. You pass the test. Now go, therefore, for I grant you safe passage through my land, and safely you may dwell west in the Isle of Balar—guards shall take you there, for your safety as well as for mine. The sword freely given I shall guard, and name it Torodagnir. May it gladly spill again the blood of trolls."

With that the Sindeldi king had sent away the two orchoth, and it was held a thing of high marvel that of that race any should have turned from evil, at least in part. They were well watched as they travelled further beyond the sight of the Dark Lord, and on their journey were questioned much about their ways. Some afterwards held that even the darkest of the Psuchai could not but have some inner spark of Eru contending against the Dark; others said nay.

∞

Silgossel it was who first sensed danger. Angruin, smarting from his wound, had soon resolved the pain, for he still had his native strength in greater part. Thus by the power of his will he had healed the weakness of his body, and flown away in rage seeking Usen's children. The children of mud could be played with another time, and this was but his maiden flight. He sought both positive results to enrich his reputation, and a diversion to stop churning over Necuratu's usurpation of his plans.

"'Ware the west wind!" The couple stared up into the skies and beheld the swift gliding descent of Angruin. Indeed, it was they who first coined his new name. Having spotted them, he decided to play with them. To the trunk of their tree he set his fire, which pierced through its girth as easily as iron sword cleaves flesh. The shaken tree shuddered in its death throes. Caliglin and Silgossel leapt from their toppling tower onto a neighbouring tree, as Angruin swooped around for another pass.

Fire singed their heads, and quickly they descended from tree to floor. Then they fled towards the Thousand Caves, towards safety. Others there were of the Sindeldi, who, met *en route* and armed with bows, sought to slay the menace of the skies. Plunging down and darting between the trees, the dragon rebuked their impertinence in flames of fury. Their swords sparkled into molten tongues, withered, and were no more. Scorched earth bore drops of burning metal, traces of bows and of arrows, but not of guards.

Other than such border patrols, few carried weapons. Harps were preferred in times of peace within the forest. The couple fled on in fear, weaponless. But Angruin was in playful mood, and didn't intend to kill these mice—let them run, that was fun. Fire rained down behind, to their left, and to their right. Scorched of skin were they, yet still they fled. Angruin disappeared, yet he plotted their path. Silently he flew ahead of them, then landed, the cat awaiting the mice. And swiftly they fled almost to his very maw. Instantly they stopped dead in their tracks. His playfulness was plain. Time to talk. "What do you seek here?" asked Caliglin.

"Child of Usen, how direct you are. Demand of me, who come from afar? Puny ones oft' lack in courtesy; since I am great, bow ye down to me. Since you did sing and you did chuckle, may I not kiss the happy couple?" Angruin stood with a cheeky grin on his unfriendly face, like to a prehistoric bird of prey.

"Flimsy we might be to you, but we are no fools. For see, it is clear that you are Ibauglir, or some mighty diaboloi of his, and that no love you have for our kind. Why stand in mockery of us, when our fate is sealed?" demanded Caliglin, protectively, pessimistically, pointlessly, standing in front of Silgossel.

That wiped the smug look off the creature's face, and the rhyme from his playtime. "To link me to him and his is unjust insult, O insolent one. And to protect the pretty one is pathetic below contempt. My fire can rip through iron; what shield is your body? But know you that I am the only one of my kind, and that your Ibauglir himself envies my skills. And who is he that I should bow down to him? He too is insolent, and mayhap one day shall feel my force." Angruin was boastful, though he knew well that his boasting was but in vain.

"Then who are you, and why did you come to kill? If you be of the Philikoi, should we not unite against the Dark Enemy?" asked Caliglin, still staying protectively in front of his belovèd.

"Come to kill? Oh certainly not! But your archers greeted me with hail of arrows. Why should I not have returned their greeting with a vengeance? Insolence must be punished, must it not? As to who I am, that I change even as my mood. Call me what you will."

"Angruin I would name you," said Silgossel standing forth, "for your fire is like a sword of iron, and a flame that cuts through iron. Yet I sense great danger, and believe not that you seek to help the free peoples of Middle-earth, whether or not you curse Ibauglir. Come now, what is your purpose here, and what would you have of us?"

"As to that, fair lady, I have said it. I would have that you bow down and worship me, for am I not glorious in being, awesome beyond praise, and great in power? Why then do you remain standing on your feet as if my equals, and not fall down prostrate before me, your heads to the ground in obeisance? As to Angruin that you name me, that is good, and by your wit you gain your life, if your companion does but bow down before me. I might even spare his insolent life, if you worship me", teased Angruin, his plans to play and slay already formed.

Such worship was a mere courtesy of bowing low in respect of a higher, a token not in itself an act of dedication or of devotion. They had no qualm against prostrating themselves before this winged creature of wondrous power, whether he was friend or foe, and bow low they did. Angruin smiled unpleasantly. "You have answered one question—how low can you bow? Now for my next—how fast can you run, my pretty mice? Run, run, as fast as you can, flee fast from the frying pan, run back to your people, so-called free, I'll burn one now, as I'm so fiery. Now shall I punish full, insolence shown me, yet leave full tearful, one to tell my glory." With that, fire spewed forth from his mouth, high above their heads.

Terrified they fled, but away from their people, for they realised that this cat must not be led down their mouse hole, and that his words spoke deliberate death to but one of them. Thus it was that Caliglin ran behind Silgossel, for their foe was chasing them, and his death would mean her life. Should Angruin overtake them, then Caliglin would run in front of Silgossel. Thus it was that when, after playtime came slaytime, Caliglin was consumed and Silgossel lived to spread word of a new terror of the skies. As a spirit unhoused, Caliglin hastened to the Halls of Mandos that stood upon the rim of the outer sea, there to sit in the shadowlands of his past, and to muse upon his future. There he would find welcome, and many would praise his nobility in yielding himself unto death. There he would await Silgossel, though he wait ever so many Ages.

THREE~   Misadelphia

As the prototype dragon, Angruin flew low through the skies, his brutal heart burning with dark pride within. His scaly skin was his delight, as brand new clothes to one grown shabby in insignificance. His fearsome shadow reflected back from the black waters of the inland Sea of Helcar, illuminated only by the undulation and effervescence of the waves beneath the full moon. The stars were twinkling bright above, yet were dark below, as if in hiding from this new reign of terror flying forth in the splendour of its pride, seeking whom it may devour. But the blood of stars was not on Angruin's mind, nor in his thoughts. His mission was to speak face to face with his brother, so that none could overhear his plan. They were a telepathic race, yet those powers, like others, were waning. He needed to be closer to communicate. Besides, face to face he could speak audibly, a safer way to talk when crucial secrets were at stake.

Thus swiftly from the west flew Angruin, over the waters, swinging slightly south. Half again the distance would take him to his brother's lair. Those were days when the world was very different than it is now. Many lands then are not now, and many lands now were not then. And west across waters a different land coexisted with that of Middle-earth, a land now long withdrawn into the unseen. That rupture between heaven and earth, was wrought by the machinations of the Dark Lord, and the Cosmic King himself now sits in silence, entering more fully into the eternal song, which weaves within itself even the death chant of the Dark Lord. Into his malevolent machinations would come the great drakes, both of the cold and of the hot. But for now, the first dragon alighted before his brother, Wayanár.

Having thrown off his alliance with the Dark Lord, Angruin knew that he must secure help from the Night. He was pleased with his first salvo in his new shape, establishing his reputation as a creator of terror among Usen's children. Would that his own people would see his greatness! Yet for all his pride, at the end of the day he was a prince—but no more than a prince. Just like Wayanár his brother, both adoptees of King Elaran. But with the help of Wayanár, he could become king: Elaran was too insular by half. Besides, Usen seemed to be allowing Necuratu the chance to break loose and to dominate Middle-earth. Why should vampires not be top of the food chain?

"Greetings, Wayanár. I have come far to see and to speak with you", said the deep gruff voluminous voice of unveiled venom.

But Wayanár was singularly unimpressed, and the stronger of the two. He'd sometimes wondered why his father had chosen Angruin for a son, and had decided that it was to keep this vampire lord under some kind of parental control. "Welcome, brother prince, for think not to deceive my old eyes with your new shape. I see behind your mask", replied Wayanár, wondering if this were some kind of test. His brother quickly returned to his default humanoid shape, and sat down. Sitting down, lying down, hanging upside down, all superfluous postures really, but they had learnt to mimic humanoids so well that sitting had become second nature. Likewise when in bat or wolf shape, they mimicked such creatures. In fact Angruin didn't merely sit down, he sprawled down, his body language saying that he was completely at ease with Wayanár.

He began a low chuckling, some inner joke no doubt tickling his fancy. By long experience Wayanár knew that that was a lead-in to being told what it was—Angruin would wish to tell more than Wayanár would wish to hear. And sure enough, after a pause of some hours, Angruin had internally relived his private little joke—time rolls slower for vampires than for mortal man doomed to die—and got down to letting his brother in on his little joke.

At last he spoke: "Today I have had such fun as I have not had for a lifetime, brother. For in my new shape I have played with the Adopted and with the Children. The former made at me with their mattocks, and I burnt their buttocks. Even you would have laughed. The latter had the temerity to fire arrows at me, but they felt fire from me in exchange. One lovely lady I sent fleeing back to her king with report of my majesty. For her part she has given me a new name, all very grand. I like it, and Angruin I shall be, one whose fire cleaves as iron—in their tongue. But alas she fled without her lover of the tree tops. They were so free, when in their tree. They smote my ire, I built their pyre", he chuckled.

Wayanár was less than amused: "Angruin, I fear, will be a name of grief. Yes, a little fun is permitted, but a little fun can go a long way, too far at times. Is it not enough for these creatures to be under peril from the

Dark Lord, that we must go and increase their fear? Are we not to keep dark our ways? And when we must reveal ourselves to them, should any survivor be left to tell? Fine, if you must raise hell now and again, blow your stack to cool down. But if your prey pray for mercy, heed it not. Yet I accuse you not of mercy, but of pride, revealing no doubt your type to the Children of Usen, to whom you should be anonymous. I fear that you are a fool", responded Wayanár, pacing up and down in vexation. Angruin's jolly joke only caused him disgruntlement. Did Angruin have a death wish? Did he wish the Kingdom of Night to collapse? Even the Sindeldin king was not to be trifled with, let alone the greater queen. In secrecy was their strength.

Angruin, often a little thoughtless when out for fun, was outwardly unperturbed. On reflection, maybe it would have been better to have let Ibauglir carry the can and the credit, instead of highlighting his hatred of him. But then again, part of the fun was giving the Children a new foe to fear, seeing them run, inciting others to fear, gaining his own name of terror. And why share his glory with another?

Anyway, he could cover it up before his brother, who would hardly hobnob with the Children to verify or falsify his defence. Wayanár was not his keeper. Most vampires practiced takiya, the art of lying, although it was supposedly meant only towards outsiders, to keep insider information inside where it belonged. "Call your brother a fool, damn you? As if! To those fools I was but a spirit of Ibauglir, escaped from the great enclosure. 'Fool' you say. No more than you. For we are both mighty among vampires, yet, like the Dark Lord, we allow these impotent imps to hem us in, the food to cage the feeder.

"Why should we not turn the tables? Why should we not join with the Dark Lord? Would he not reward us for releasing him from his captivity? I know that he is planning to soon break free—indeed I might even have given him some ideas—but what if we do not side with him? Once he has put down his enemies, might he not seek some special reward for those who have not aided him in his righteous cause?" In pride Angruin had swung away from Necuratu, now in pride he swung back.

"Angruin, Elaran our father-king has forbidden any alliance with the Necrotic Kingdom. Indeed, he has pondered whether we should ally against it. For the Dark Lord proves treacherous even to his friends—it is his nature. What care of us has he who neither needs blood nor body?

You seek short-term gain, but if we plunder our reserves now, what will we drink when all blood has run dry?" Wayanár was more perturbed than ever. A madcap shenanigan against the Adopted and the Children, might be harmless folly—like smashing a few eggs—but the talk had become treasonable.

"Wayanár, Elaran our father-king has veered towards the Light, therefore he is dangerous, do you not see that? Are we not adopted to aid him? What greater help can we provide except to protect him from the Light, by steering him towards the Dark, stabilising him?" Angruin was no longer lounging around, but like Wayanár was pacing up and down, his body mirroring his inner agitation. Perhaps his opening gambit had been unwise. It would not be easy to escape Wayanár.

But, in for a penny, in for a pound. "Do you not agree that siding with our food is inherently wrong, indeed perverse? How can you agree with our father, then? Is it not wrong that he even speaks such thoughts to us? And how could we align with the Children without revealing ourselves, which conflicts with our core policy of concealment? Does he not sink his own boat by such meditations? Besides, if you dare not ally with the Necros, why then, why should we not simply stand aside and let the Children battle the Necros to the death? Will we not then be stronger than the winning side, able to defeat it?"

"Angruin, these are matters for the king. To counsel him is one thing; to rebel against him is another. Is it for naught that he is our king?" asked Wayanár.

"Was it for naught that we became princes?" shot back Angruin. "Cannot you see? We can profit by the Dark Lord's confinement—either as allies or as neutrals—or lose as enemies. Choose either good, and your choice shall be mine. Only choose not the way of the Children, for I shall gainstay you."

"Bold words, my brother prince, which I think you would be hard pressed to fulfil", muttered Wayanár. He was not a vampire to be intimidated by a mere show of power, and he judged spirits mainly by their thelodynamic stature. Sadly the world was changing, and he was slow to change with it. He failed to see how outward appearances could win allies and daunt enemies, and how skills could be used in internecine battle—it could prove deadly to let Angruin depart in peace, but should he have slain him there and then?

What he did see, were three salient facts. One, that one to one, Angruin was but a defeated foe in his hands, whether shaped as a winged worm, or as a wily wolf. Two, though the outcome was assured, to capture or kill Angruin would bloody both—and only a fool would rush in where aggeloi would fear to tread. He saw success through blood: so what? But the third thing he saw held back his hand. For he saw that private victory could be kingdom defeat. For to incinerate or indict his brother risked civil war, which for him meant substantial bickering between individuals, resulting in many deaths and a diminution of power, in turn exposing their kingdom to a takeover bid by the Dark Lord, as he controlled the orchoth.

Even if the Dark Lord held back—he had his own problems—civil war would be followed by an extensive recovery time for the kingdom. Did the kingdom really need a bloodletting at this time? In fact, if Angruin were brought before the Great Council, even it might even be swayed by him, especially if learning that Elaran had expressed tendencies towards the Children of Usen. A live Angruin posed problems any way you looked at it. Royals were not permitted to go live with inside information, but Angruin might, and the king might die. The king had as yet only bounced that idea off his sons, but it wouldn't do to tell the Great Council even that! Alas, the Night Kingdom was hitting a bad patch, for the passive policy of Elaran was causing stresses and strains within his kingdom. Now that unease was bothering the two brothers.

Wayanár just couldn't see that by looking good as a winged worm, Angruin could gain followers of fashion, and so could eventually overthrow Wayanár. In those days, vampires simply did not think like that, for to date they lacked any corporate enemy to establish an army against, or private enemies to warrant bodyguards. Their only fight was against those of the Dawn, and that fight was completely *ad hoc*.

The Dark Lord, a skilled master of solid matter, manipulating the very flesh and bones of Arda, dwelt within an impregnable volcanic fortress, its power subject to his will—he had it easy but his pride sought more. Though the Necrotic Kingdom lay dormant, pressure was building up within the Night lord's kingdom—uncontrollable tremors, the venting of pent up fumes, a bubbling forth of burning anger. Angruin was but one—though probably the chief—agitator.

Perhaps Wayanár should have had it out with Angruin there and then. But he did not.

Their *tête-à-tête* had pleased neither, and had been a tad inflamed. It had even mooted the overthrow of the king, and the brothers ruling the kingdom together. Arrant nonsense churned out in the fit of rage. Choosing monarchs was for the Great Council, not for usurpers, and regicide spelt death for villains and victims alike. That they could cover it up, accuse the Kingdom of Dawn as having sent the assassin, or present it as self-defence—as if a mad king had tried to spear his chief musician and been speared himself—also came into what only the ultra-polite might call 'the conversation'. That 'conversation' had soon degenerated into a shouting match, a slanging match, producing more heat than light. Wayanár's determination not to lay into Angruin, was tested to its limits, and none too soon did Angruin depart in peace, who should perhaps have stayed in pieces. Perhaps the only good that had come out of it was that both brothers knew where the other stood. That could help one to prepare defence, the other to prepare attack.

Angruin flew off into the night sky in search of a strong ally. Into the far north he flew, easing his mind, cooling down his wrath, collecting his thoughts. He realised that he had said too much, and knew that he could be dragged before the Great Council to answer the serious charge of regicide, for the very idea was deemed as guilt. However his brother was slow on the uptake, and would surely sit on things—a vampire of more thought than action. Therein lay his salvation, for he could strike first while the iron was hot—was that not his new name? This time he flew high, but not above the peaceful illuminated blue cloud cover, a sign of noctilucent numbness above—in stark contrast to the mid-summer madness below. He would get even. Resisting the temptation to swiftly descend to terrorise more of the Children—business before pleasure—he approached his destination, flying lower, searching for the vampire duke of that domain: he had worked with him before.

Life is seldom so simple. Duke Fangli had disappeared, though not without trace. Even a vampire cannot disappear into thin air, although invisibility—though a costly cloak—could be donned in great need. Angruin began his search, crisscrossing the multiyear ice:

albedo levels were high in that area, and life was cooling down. Soon he met with two vampires, both feasting on a recently captured Child—feasts becoming a rare treat in the north. At first sight of him they tried to flee, one flying west, one fleeing east.

Quickly he outpaced the one to the east, and brought her down with a resounding bolt. She lay splayed out on the ice, breathing heavily, expecting no mercy. The law of Elaran was clear: hands off the Children. And here was a son of Elaran, come doubtless to enforce his law and to punish with a heavy hand any transgressor. Never before had enforcers come into the far north, and the northerners had not felt any need of any great secrecy.

Their own duke was favourably lax over that law, indeed it was rumoured that he himself had been the first to transgress it—and it was good. Now expecting no mercy, she was shown none, yet he spared her life nonetheless. Indeed he commended her defiance of the king. For while the king disallowed the Children from the menu, he did so simply out of fear, fear that if outsiders molested the Children, Usen would awake in wrath.

Funny, vampires still thought of themselves as incomers, though they had arrived before the world was fully formed, when it was merely swung around by the music of deep heaven, like a common pebble in a sling. But Angruin believed that the fear of Usen was the end of wisdom: live without any affirming of the tyrant; live as you will. Fear not, believe in yourself, and you will see the glory of greatness. This defiance the wench before him had, and he respected her for it. Yet she could not tell him where her lord had gone, except that he had sneaked away like a thief into the night. To Angruin that suggested only one thing. He left her, and flew off into the night sky.

Meanwhile Wayanár had privately reported back to his royal father. "My lord, I bring ill tidings of great woe. Alas I fear treachery, treachery from Prince Angruin—as your son now styles himself. Behold, he has taken on a new shape, and has already used it in aggression towards the Children, and itches to ramp up hostility towards them. His thoughts are confused, but tend towards taking the crown of this kingdom. He cares not whether Necuratu wins or loses, but would as happily support him as stand aloof. He threatens to proclaim publicly your private thoughts, for he abhors even the thought of aligning with the Light."

A son could be a great asset, but also a great danger. So should the king agree with Angruin—the policy of appeasement: peace in our time, whatever comes after? It would keep the king and sons onboard, but not in good conscience. Or should he ignore him and press forward? At best the king and one son would remain onboard. But getting the Great Council onboard with a pro-Light scheme, a pro-Life scheme, was chancy. Bigotry towards the Light was strong with the Dark Side. Elaran might well be dethroned, perhaps banished, in which case his deliberations would die with his reign. Then what? Wayanár, if he became king, would have to adopt a neutral stance, which Angruin had allowed to be an acceptable option, and Angruin would perhaps become his son. On the other hand, the Great Council might enthrone Angruin, in which case a pro-Necros stance was almost inevitable, whether sooner or later, for that seemed to be Angruin's endgame.

So the three kingdom-options were perhaps deliverance (Elaran), danger (Wayanár), or disaster (Angruin). If baggage risked sinking the ship, should it not be thrown overboard? What if Angruin were that baggage? If he must be drowned, he must be drowned quickly, he and his ideas, before mutiny spread among the crew: kill quietly; kill swiftly. Assassination was fraught with danger, but the king decided that elimination offered the best solution. If he worked with Wayanár, it shouldn't be too hard. He wondered whether he would be well advised to adopt a wise daughter to replace a wayward son. It was the way of both Pneumata and Powers to adopt—sometimes reimaging their children—for they could not breed except through the Psuchai.

Four

*E*T TU BRUTE?

When not in ectoplasmic mode, diaboloi are generally invisible to the Children, who on the spirit-plane have no eyes to see. But to the inner eyes of the Pneumata, they are always visible as kindred spirits, for their sight delves deep beyond the mortal boundaries of light. If the Kingdom of Night had lost a lord, a lord who held loose to his king, then likely enough the Kingdom of Necros would be in the know. In search of his alter ego Fangli, Angruin sought out the local dunamos, guessing that he had probably hired him to go undercover.

So it was that Angruin soon learnt that a secondborn Children had awoken far in the southeast, seemingly of lesser consequence than the firstborn. Runts of Usen? But according to the dunamos, these secondborn must not be allowed to gang up with the firstborn against the Necros. Already their strengths and weaknesses were being analysed. Along with diaboloi, Necuratu himself had been hands on on the job, whispering unseen among this race. He was now recruiting discreet vampires to be tangible assets in corrupting this new people, speaking in the days while his diaboloi spoke in the nights, so night and day playing around with their heads, messing with their minds.

These Children certainly had plenty of weaknesses, and Usen had surely shot himself in the foot by sporting death as a special gift. Death had always seemed a good way to inspire fear and resentment. Many fools seemed to think that they had a right to life, in which case woe betide any who tried to deprive them of their so-called right, even Usen himself! Calling death a gift—as if a blessing, not a curse—could be rubbished as doubletalk. It was doom, clear and simple, as any fool could see. There was a lot to play with, and the job to spread disaffection, should be easy.

Happily, besides being easy victims to death, this secondborn spawn seemed prone to aches and pains not native to the firstborn. And unlike the firstborn, they had had no call unto undying West-over-Waters—were they unloved, abandoned children? If a child asks for a fish, would a father give it a snake; if it asked for a rattle, would he give it a rattlesnake? Not if a loving father, unless he was a fool. Usen was no fool, therefore he was unloving—saying otherwise was a blatant lie.

If the firstborn apprehended this axiom, they would abandon him and be swiftly saved by dark realism. So this creation of new life, had breathed new life into the Necros, long starved of good news. At last a new game was afoot; time to let slip. If Usen promised death, diaboloi promised a fight. A fight against the firstborn and against Usen, or even with the firstborn against Usen—a dream ticket.

Or, disturbing thought, was Usen being more subtle than a snake? Was he wily enough to deceive, if possible, the very Necros? Could death have a secret sting? Was it all just too easy, like juicy bait to a fish? Might they be caught out, left floundering high and dry? No! As the dunamos said, recruiting vampires would offer rich reward, guarantee success, and humiliate Usen.

Necuratu couldn't work with a hesitant king, but would love to work with the king's son—the dunamos obviously hadn't heard about Angruin's fallout with Necuratu! Necuratu had already secretly summoned the duke of the northern territories, and the mission was simple: inspire the secondborn to worship the Necros, to turn away from the Light. Convince them that Usen the Unfair, had made them mortal as some kind of punishment for uncommitted crimes, that they were born blind, so to speak, for Usen's glory. Already Necuratu himself had invisibly moved among them, laying the seeds of corruption. So spoke the dunamos.

Angruin could read the mind of the Dark Lord—hope, doubt, recruitment. The dunamos had hinted that for services rendered, there would be payment in blood, besides a palpable hit against Usen, and goodwill among diaboloi. And if a vampire eventually aligned with the Kingdom of Necros, then possible promotion up the ranks? Since the Necros was rising, why not join with that Power, rise with it, perhaps rise through it?

Indeed he was tempted. If Wayanár had joined with him, together they might well have taken up the implied offer. Truth be told, Angruin was a little concerned about taking up with the Kingdom of Necros on his own, since he feared that his anger at Necuratu might surface, endangering his life if unaided. He refused to admit the mindboggling power of Necuratu, far beyond mere dunamoi, far beyond princes of the Night.

Though not understanding his indecision, the dunamos directed him to the Vale of Sleep within a land of two mighty rivers, wherein the secondborn had awoken, a little south from where the firstborn had awoken. It was surpassing strange that both Children had awoken far in the east, when the chief Guardians lived so far in the west. If it meant that Usen did not wish to protect his children well, well then he deserved to lose a fair few, didn't he? It was a happy thought for Angruin. Buoyed up from his confabulation, he again roared into the skies, looking to touch base with Fangli.

Under a full moon it wasn't long before he had spotted him, had landed in his dragon shape, and had offered the duke future promotion—if only he would join with him. Fresh from battle, Fangli was full of news and quite animated. He had been secretly under cover for some time, and could report good news to his boss. The Children he had been put in charge of, had largely swallowed the line that Usen's gift was a gift of spite and slavery. That Usen favoured his firstborn far more. That therefore, to prevent the secondborn being able to exceed them in skill and power through longevity, in fear he had imposed extremely short mortal spans on them, so that they would be short-lived slaves of the firstborn, mere puppets, howbeit handy puppets.

Given the nod, they had soon seen through Usen's designs, and raised hell. They had marched into the land where the firstborn had awoken, and symbolically raised their flag of protest and rebellion. Delectably—and almost as good as total rebellion against the Light— some of the secondborn had rebelled against the rebels. Infighting was delightful news to deliver to the Dark Lord, Lord of Confusion. Fortunately it was only a small percentage of the secondborn, and Fangli predicted that that lot would never in a million years amount to much, neither use nor ornament in the history of Middle-earth, at best a soon forgotten joke. The incredulous idea that one day the secondborn would rule the earth, was a load of sheer baloney.

Nevertheless, having led his first fight, Fangli looked favourably on ditching Necuratu to fight for a vampire cause. And he had tasted new blood. He had always had a penchant to taste the Children's blood. Like a connoisseur, he could discuss the finer differences between bloods. The Children's far exceeded the blood of the Phusika—even the Children of Mud was a little richer than theirs!—but the blood of the secondborn was only a little lower than the excellent vintage of the firstborn's, and a lot less hazardous to obtain. It had been part of the promise made by the dunamos of the north, and had been well worth a little effort in troublemaking. "Angruin, come, let your business wait. The victors of Palisor have many victims, secondborn who await now the Gift of Usen. Yet before their spirits flee, let us drink to our fill. You will join me, surely?" Angruin didn't need to be asked a second time.

A kin-slaying had ended in the defeat of Usen and the irreversible mastery for Necuratu, and the Night Kingdom could boast its part. Speedily Angruin flew forth with Fangli to the field of battle. There there were many bodies of the slain, including bodies of some species whose blood he disdained to taste, and some of the mud-born whose blood was as a cheap wine. Of the secondborn he needed not the slain, for the captured would prove the tastier to his palate. Casting business aside, they threw themselves into blood frenzy, biting living breathing shrieking bodies without let or hindrance, while the host stood by and watched.

Oh and what a feast it was, and how content they were when finally they were crop set, fair brussen, full to bursting. Those who had survived their rampage were now thrown to the black skinned slaves of Necuratu, and to his wolves. Even those they had drained to death, now—though they never knew it—had their earthly remains torn apart and eaten raw. Necuratu seldom allowed his slaves such feasts, and they tended to be underfed. The vampire lords looked on with placid faces of complacent *bons viveurs*, well contented by their own feast. Soon only raw bones remained, even those somewhat gnawed. Fangli's army were gutted that some foes had escaped west, but they could always follow—Fangli would leave no foe standing!

Angruin hadn't been bothered: "Come Fangli, let us do business while the rabble feasts. I seek a strong ally to fight for mastery of the Night. For—and speak not to any other unless you are with me, else you will speak your last—our kingdom is on a knife edge. The king is corrupted by the Light, and contemplates alliance with the firstborn against

Necuratu. Necuratu we neither wish nor need, yet is infinitely to be preferred by any vampire of sense and taste. I have sounded out Wayanár, and while untainted, he is loyal to the disloyal, therefore must be opposed. Together we could defeat him, and then overthrow the king. What think you?" asked Angruin, expecting no opposition after an indulgent feast.

Fangli had recently acquired a new reason to wish Elaran dead— human blood, fresh and easy. It offered an inexhaustible supply for hungry vampires, yet only over Elaran's dead body. "I like it fine, but it must be targeted assassination, not open war. We must deliver our people, not divide them. But getting within striking reach of our targets might prove problematic. A pity perhaps that I have Children's blood on my hands, since from what I see in your mind, your father considers favouring the Children, and your brother would not disfavour them. Our partaking of the Children might now keep us beyond reach of Elaran, if he hears."

They sat a while in silent deliberation. Necuratu could be asked to help, adding muscle to their plot, but that would spark off civil war for sure. Neither wished that. Fangli's part in Palisor could be hushed up for a while, but murder will out, and any whisper of the truth— before Elaran was overthrown—could land the plotters in deep water. The typical way around that was to meet the problem head on, get one's confession in first, mixed of course with lies, so that when truth arrived it would be treated as a lie. Blame the other guy before you're blamed! An early lie makes truth too late!

What about repentance, not real, for that would never do, but a phoney change of heart and mind? "Fangli, think why you could favour the Light. Think heretical thoughts, so that by infiltration we might end heresy once and for all. If Elaran could be persuaded that you had forsaken the Dark Way and become susceptible to the Light, he could overlook your work for Necuratu and welcome you as a convert and confidante. Then, glorious irony, you could stab him in the back, as I stab from the front." Bit by bit a plan was strung together, which would reward Fangli with a princedom, should Angruin become king.

Angruin then made himself scarce, leaving no hint that he had met with Fangli, nor even sought for him. Fangli meanwhile went as a penitent unto the king. "My king, strike me down, for I come fresh from a work of Necuratu. Behold, an embassage from the Dark Lord came to me in the far north, promising fresh and fulsome supplies for my people, in return for a trifling yet sensitive errand to the southeast by the eastern sea. In folly I went, believing my task merely to spread dissention among the Children towards Usen. Alas for my folly, for the Dark Lord planned both their death and to bloody my unwilling hands. For I have long held the blood of the Children to be precious in the sight of Usen, and though I love him not, his Children are sacred to me.

"Against my will a war was fought, grieving my heart to have been enmeshed in that foul web. Dastardly the Dark Lord then feigned to reward my people with Usen's children, that we might fatten them for slaughter. That cuisine I could never countenance, and knowing that he knew it full well and so mocked me as a fool, I fled from him in bitterness, and will serve him no more. My king, at last I realise that his ways lead to bad death, and since he is the enemy of the Children, I even wonder whether we should strengthen the Children against him, the father of lies and lord of flies. But that very thought is evil! Guilty of such delinquent thought, I surely must not be spared, for I have both served Necuratu, and looked towards the Light—a double sin. Which is the greater, I know not, but both must surely be punished, and I throw myself upon your justice for the good of our people." Thus Fangli feigned virtue and lied in vice.

Best kept in the dark that he knew from Angruin that the king had thought thoughts of the Light and pondered over supporting the Children. *I know that you know that I know that you know*, gets rather complicated. Besides, an ace in the hand might prove useful to play before the Great Council. Carefully the king questioned him further, and so learned of a new kind of Child, the secondborn.

Then the wisdom of Necuratu was made clear: to strike while the iron was hot, to sow discord before concord could be fashioned. Elaran saw that one of his lords, having played a part in that (Fangli minimised his part), could complicate his nascent plans, but a true convert could contribute to them. Had this been reported to him by anyone else, his hand would have been heavy upon the offender. However, Necuratu's tool had been troubled over Necuratu's treachery, and had only complied to help his own people, his motivation being pure. That's what Elaran wished to believe, and he believed as he wished.

Fangli was good, thought Elaran, who of late had been radically rethinking the whole idea, good.

Whence came the good? Was it sourced from the Light? If Usen was at the centre, did that then mean that Usen was goodness, defining what was good and what was not? Usen's own children had puzzled over that, too. Some had said that the good was a self-existent standard and totally independent of Usen, in which case Usen prescribed the good under its compulsion and was himself judged by it. Others said that no independent standard could judge the independent Usen, else Usen was not in fact independent. They argued that he himself had merely invented, out of his own head, what should be good for his creatures. Their argument could mean that good was simply an outcome of his arbitrary choice: would murder have been good had he chosen it to be, and medicine evil? Could it have been otherwise?

To deny that it could have been otherwise, would be to say that Usen was under a compulsion—the alternative idea, rather than having perfectly unforced choice. But what if neither idea was right? What if he simply demanded of others what he himself was—perfect harmony—that *good* was consonant with his being? Since morality was a society thing, would that mean that Usen was the eternal uncreated society—not the eternal person? If so, how could he logically be defined as evil? Could in fact the Eighth Law somehow be defended as good, if all were known?

These thoughts, almost infinitely slow to reluctantly trickle through, were now asking whether the balance of power should shift to an intrinsic right, the Light, and the Dark left. In questioning his past dogmatism, he had come to doubt himself, but was perhaps too prone to believe any who seemed to truly second his metaphysical soul-searching. Too easy to pin praise, rather than blame, on one who seemingly had joined the same road, or at least looked longingly at it. Would he blame himself?

Now by deception, the enemy was within. Fangli had entered the king's counsel, rather than the king's *calabozo*. Meanwhile, Angruin remained at large, not donning his dragon shape so as to lie low, while as a bat silently stalking the firstborn who besieged the Dark Lord, taking as his hidden home a cave within the Blue Mountains. He left alone the Adopted, because their blood was unsavoury, and more so because he wished his hiddenness to remain hidden. Only Fangli knew of his whereabouts. So it remained until the Dark Lord's first dragon arose upon the earth, filling the firstborn with fear as he crept along unstoppable. Urnúla had done her work. For from her womb had come a worm, a hideous distortion of nature, a creature that could multiply after its own kind, and he became also the first father of dragons. Unknown to Elaran, Angruin the first dragon fathered no offspring, sheathed his shape, and waited.

Long had the mother of Necuratu's dragon forged his genes by her will, taking and reshaping DNA sequences from her unhappy mates. In a world of trial and error, many errors there had been, until the Dark Lord was satisfied with the fruit of her womb. Long did that fruit live awaiting the light of that day, when it would be allowed to come forth from the earth in glorious splendour, to the dismay of his enemies. Patience was not his lot, and in disobedience he had come forth from the dark fortress too soon, believing himself unassailable. And for a time it had seemed so. He was the first dragon of the Dark Lord, and history would by and large forget the vampire lord from whence came the slithery shape into Necuratu's dark mind. Yet it would remember how Urnúla's son was soon humbled by the firstborn, and limped back to his dark master, tail between his legs. A daughter too had his mother born, and from brother and sister would come forth a bastard brood with thelodynamic power enough to daunt and dismay even the Guardians, for they hosted the greater of the Turannoi as symbiotics, invisible riders on visible steeds— diabolical dragons. Yet Elaran waited not for their wrath to appear.

A mighty dragon had come forth, and in Elaran's mind Angruin was the only suspect. Angruin had hitherto disappeared from the face of the earth. Wayanár had enlisted the aid of mighty eagles, but the labile lord remained elusive even from their piercing eyes. Fangli knelt before the king: "If I have favour in your sight, my lord, permit me to return to my dukery, for it might be that the rebel hides far away in the north. My people are loyal to me as to the king, and it might be that I shall find news of his lurkings."

Scarcely a hundred winters had flown by, but Elaran had come to trust his new counsellor. To send him on a mission to his people, would both explore a region where the rebel might lay hid, and affirm his trust in Fangli. Thus it was that taking a chance, he permitted him to return to his powerbase. Thus it was that Fangli flew straight to where he knew Angruin to be, checking of course that no unfriendly eyes were following him. Thus it was that he and Angruin soon plotted the king's death—dealing with Wayanár could wait. Elaran would be told that Angruin's lair was discovered, and that a snatch and grab op was needed: if they were to sting like a bee they must first fly like a butterfly. If the element of surprise was lost, Angruin might well escape to some other hiding place, of which apparently he had several. Therefore, let it be heralded that the king had sent a host of vampires to the Iron Hills to capture the rebel. Then Fangli and Elaran could quietly sneak up unawares to slay the dragon.

To be a king meant to be a warrior, and Elaran fancied his chances against Angruin the Brute. With Fangli's aid, victory was in the bag. Wayanár had begged in vain to escort the king; "three's a crowd", countered Fangli. And so it was that without guards they journeyed together to the Blue Mountains, where the tables were turned. Fangli went as a bat from hell; Elaran as a lamb to the slaughter.

The radical belief of Angruin was clear. The Necros was right; the Light was wrong. His king, having considered a false move towards the Light, should be deposed for the good of the kingdom. This both justified regicide and justified double dealing. Fangli had agreed, had had dealings with the Necros, had willingly partaken of the blood of the firstborn and of secondborn of Usen. Angruin's big brother had been too lily-livered to join the plan, so in turn should die. The trap had been laid. Hunter and executioner silently approached.

"My lord, you must now be as silent as a sheep before shearers, for we are very close." They resumed humanoid form, and crept quietly up the slopes. All was quiet on the western front. Even birds had forsaken this patch of deadness. Apart from some wind in the willows—there was a mere on the eastern slopes—no sound was to be heard. Fangli, whether intentionally or unintentionally, switched from leading the way to being led. The cave was in sight, and Elaran was eager to engage his enemy. So it was that Elaran first entered the cavern, spacious inside and replete with stalagmites and stalactites.

There was a drip drip drop, plonk plonk plink, as water fell into dark pools within. Dark was of course but light to vampires, being used to living in the dark. To eyes that could see beyond the electromagnetic spectrum's white light, the colours were both beautiful and restful. It was not for nothing that nowadays they preferred to travel at night or under cloud of day. To their highly trained noses the psychic scent of vampires lingered, wafting from the nether regions of the cave complex, where their prey seemingly lurked. Quietly they stalked their game. Yet he too was aware of them. Although their scent did not flow towards him, their psychic resonance could be felt, all the more because he was expecting them. Still he awaited them and stirred not.

Angruin had offered Fangli a sonship, on the proviso of course that he himself was elected to be king. Both were reasonable prospects— had Fangli come as friend? It was unlikely but possible that Elaran— or Wayanár for that matter—might have made a similar offer, which could have tempted Fangli to betray him. But Fangli was, like himself, opposed as a matter of principle, to any idea of opening up to the

Light, and Necuratu was their best bet in keeping that door closed. Their only viable choice was to help the Dark Lord—or at least to sit back and let him fight his own battles. It was true that he was confined to his own fortress, as if under house arrest, but he was planning a massive breakout, and once out, the Children would be scattered and scarred into subjection. It was only a matter of time. No, Fangli would not betray him, for Necuratu was odds on to win. Soon it would be the end of the Night as they had long known it. Any minute now Elaran would feel a knife in his back—the betrayer of the waning Night would be betrayed by the darker Night, poetic justice.

∞

King Elaran had left with Fangli, leaving Wayanár in the arms of anxiety, for he just could not shake off a sense of impending doom. Although the report had been that Angruin was alone, what if he had picked up allies, perhaps vampires or diaboloi? That could make it nigh on impossible to defeat him by a small scale attack. Elaran had great power, sizeably more than the powerful Fangli. Angruin sat somewhere between the two, so the two against him—if only him— should be a doddle. And yet, and yet. If the king's guess was right, then the recently unveiled dragon was Angruin.

In which case, since the dragon was Necuratu's pet, was it not likely that he now networked with diaboloi? Though if so, it was curious as to why he would be dwelling in the Blue Mountains, rather than in the Iron Mountains with his master! Might the Dark Lord in fact have been busy building up secret power bases beyond the siege, bases that could help him to break free? Yet Fangli had been confident about his intel. Something didn't add up. Finally yielding to his disquiet, Wayanár raced rapidly across the skies to the only one of the mighty whom he trusted more than life itself, Rátek. Within the kingdom she was a noble—though she claimed that within the region of the seven dimensions she was a royal, the princess of Bulika.

At that time she dwelt nearby, at least in body. She was special, and she was strange, something of a visionary. According to her she did not transgress the Eighth Law, but simply played within its confines, exploring hidden regions within its scope. It was (she said) as if when her body rested in repose, she often descended into sub-dimensions, living there as a princess of fear, a princess not of hearts but of horror, often shapeshifting into a spotted leopard seeking blood. If her testimony was true, then other creatures there are that we cannot contact in our dimension of the universe—are there magical (or spiritual?) bridges that connect?

Could, just conceivably, our images which we see in mirrors, have lives of their own when we walk away, only appearing as mirror images when we look at them? Could there be sub-dimensional copies of our dimension, people lacking the personality properties of us, yet looking like us? Could Ectype, the twin of Archetype, have the appearance without the attitude? Might the copy-you, live in my copy-body, and the copy-I, in your copy-body? Who is to say? Rátek? At best she gave out hints, as if her hidden dominion should remain her exclusive domain. Well, it seems that Rátek had learned how to enter these deeper dimensions. Or perhaps it was simply a gift, although if it was it seemed to be a gift that no other vampire shared.

Or perhaps—some sceptics said quietly behind her back—it was only real in her dreams. Well if so it was unlike normal dreams, for causes there—she said—had effects that continued beyond waking. Not that vampires sleep as the secondborn sleep. Only their bodies needed— increasingly more—sleep; their minds stayed perfectly awake. All except Rátek's, it seemed. But then again one could say that even then her mind never slept but was simply awake in a different dimension. It was universally acknowledged that under the creator, creatures could be sub-creators, and that even as above reality there is suprareality (more substantial), so below it there was subreality (less substantial)—a holiday realm of imagination. Yet she insisted that she herself entered sub-dimensions, no more imaginary than solid earth—and she was known to be honest. Rátek was a mystic, and as level-headed a vampire as you might wish to meet.

Wayanár freely entered her cave, and was pleased to find her wide awake to the sensible world. "Hail Rátek. I come in haste, fearing for the life of our king. He has gone alone, except for Fangli, to the lair of Angruin, for Fangli has urged the power of surprise. Yet I fear some mischief, and would follow against permission of my king. Choose swiftly, but if you dare, then fly with me there, to the Blue Mountains. We must follow the psychic breezes of the king, yet not be seen unless to save him." Knowing and trusting him well, without ado she immediately joined him in his mission. Together they sped towards the mountains in the north and west, soon picking up the trail.

Yet Elaran and Fangli had outflown the wind, and before them loomed the cave entrance. There was a sense of having arrived just too soon—the air was not right. Entering the cavern, Elaran had moved slowly and cautiously, tailgated by Fangli. Around a corner he had come face to face with his errant son. "Father, welcome. Honoured I am that you come to see me, who so often has come to see you. To what do I owe this honour?"

"Alas my son, all too clear it is to me that you have resumed your shape in allegiance to the Dark Lord, endangering your people by rash action", Elaran sighed.

"You lie!" expostulated Angruin, "for the dragon of which you speak is not I but a creation of Necuratu, a shape stolen from me, for which you alone have given me credit. I thank you for that, yet you must now die, for you have rebelled towards the Light." With that Angruin, in humanoid shape, shot out a bolt of bright coquelicot flame. That, the king parried, and returned a hot bolt of alizarin, pitching Angruin backwards. Yet he himself stumbled forwards in a cry of agony, as a fork of dark violet pierced his heart from behind.

Raising himself, a bolt of coquelicot power seared through his defences, piercing his chest. He had been blindsided, after which he never recovered. Some energy bolts of his will he threw at Fangli, judging Fangli's sin the greater—for he had acted as friend and backstabber. Never would he tell him that upon Angruin's death the sonship would have been his. Only Wayanár had been told that. It would not have made any difference. His body broke from his will and perished, and as a naked spirit he departed this world, being sucked into the ethereal dimension of Usen, the judge of all judges.

Wayanár and Rátek swooped into the cave only minutes too late. The assassins were rejoicing, dead to the world around. Suddenly they were corned by two vampires mightier than they. To fight was to die, although in death they might take down one. But why should they wish to? They were not vindictive, and were unhappy to take the life of their own kind except to protect their kingdom—or their own skins. Sincerely wrong perhaps, but at least sincere. Fight being hopeless, they meekly surrendered. Besides, justice might yet pronounce in their favour, proclaiming them as heroes of the Night. And if so, royal promotion was still on the cards. The body which Elaran had had, was no more: he had been of the fire clan.

Soon guards and prisoners were assembled before a special session of the Great Council. "Angruin," said Gjaku sternly, "it is deep sorrow to try a prince for the murder of his father-king, but your story will be heard fairly. Why have you done such a thing?" Being telepathic, even normal vampires could have some inkling of the hearts of others, and members of the Great Council were particularly sensitive. Therefore they needed not to ask if, but simply why?

"Great Council, I ask for full justice. Elaran had undermined the throne by thoughts of the Light. To herald this publicly might have led to civil conflict, therefore I took it upon myself to purge our kingdom of this dross. Far from punishing me, you should promote me: I shall take the seat of he whom I deposed, and so affirm our neutrality, and perhaps enrich our friendship with the Dark Side, to the despite of Usen and to our enrichment. For the winds of change move swiftly from the east, and Necuratu has already feasted us with the blood of the secondborn." With that, Angruin urged that the restrictions imposed by Elaran should lapse by his death, opening up a new and rich supply of blood. And unless offended—and especially if served—Necuratu would strengthen their hand against any backlash from Usen.

Fangli confessed that he himself had been the first to break the ruling of King Elaran, and had feasted on the blood of the slain Children in the northwest, and later with Angruin had feasted upon the secondborn in the southeast. "Neither feasting has brought down the wrath of Usen, though would have brought down the wrath of Elaran. Is the moral not clear? Usen either cares not, else is too afraid or powerless to revenge his own, and therefore Elaran's fears were needless and showed his timidity or betrayal towards the Light. Since by our hand he is gone, have we not freed those who were held in slavery by their fear of death? Ours should be exaltation, not execution. And since Wayanár and Rátek have brought us here in chains, let them be led out in chains, for it is unbecoming that the guilty should leave scot-free."

Much was discussed, not least Wayanár's position relative to the Children and Necuratu. "Vampires only for vampires", said he, strict neutrality. True, he added, the blood of the Children seemed up for grabs, but if Usen was unwilling or unable to revenge them, then they needed not Necuratu for protection. Fine, thank the rebels for opening the door, then punish them for regicide—that was wrong whatever rights ensued. He counselled stern punishment: for Angruin, banishment in life; for Fangli, banishment from life. Had Elaran's last act not been to seek the death of Fangli? To spare his life would dishonour the former king. Unexpectedly Rátek had interrupted, begging for Fangli's life, for she claimed one of her vision things—that he would yet serve well the Kingdom of Night. Wayanár's face said it all—her flights of fantasy had gotten the better of her yet again!

All was considered, weighed up by the Great Council networking their minds together, until they came to one mind, one voice. And by the voice of Gjaku they spoke. "Angruin, your motives are judged to be pure, and your action heroic. Therefore you have our gratitude, and your life shall be spared. Nevertheless, your action can be comprehended, but cannot be condoned. Should we countenance a precedent for regicide, let alone promote the perpetrator? By no means! Therefore we must punish. You have been a prince, and have conspired with a duke. These titles we place beyond your reach, and forbid you ever to attain while this council endures. Of lesser rank you shall be, and as count you shall stand, reflecting both our approval and disapproval.

"Fangli, by the special pleading of Rátek your life too shall be spared, although we judge you with greater displeasure: your treason was dishonourable as a friend; Angruin's was honourable as an enemy. Never again will you hold noble rank within our kingdom, let alone the royal rank you have sought. You have patently sided with Necuratu, and perhaps to him you should go. But from this council you will be scourged, and held in contempt by this kingdom, as long as this council endures.

"Wayanár, in former times other candidates might have sought the throne, but this day we have with one mind agreed to bestow it on you, adopted son of Elaran. Your moderation between Dawn and Necros we affirm, and do praise your willingness to disobey your king in order to protect him. We know of no objections to calling you our king and to living by your word. By your acceptance this day, the kingdom can be saved from doubt as to our way." Gjaku sat down, and Wayanár arose.

"Gjaku, Great Council. With honour I accept this great honour, and speak now as your king. My name I shall change in token of new office, and Nindara I shall be until my death. You have vouchsafed the lives of the guilty, yet as king I may still within that limit pronounce sentence. What more can be meted out towards Fangli, besides banishment from my kingdom? And as he has schemed in cahoots with Angruin, so I banish both from my kingdom while my kingship endures. As for Rátek, by whose pleading the traitor's head is now sacred, she is well accounted wise—but this I cannot fully ignore. No positive punishment shall be hers, but negative punishment she shall know. But for her pleading she would this day have become my daughter-princess. If she will she may remain as counsellor, but she shall never dwell within my house as kin." A sceptic of prophecy, he spoke in foolish anger.

Soon all was done, and little more need be told of those days. Fangli had fled under whips of fire from the Council. Angruin had followed in their wake, able thus to help in the recovery of his servant—for that is what Fangli had become. Prince Angruin had now become Count Angruin, and Duke Fangli had been reduced into commonality. Both being banished, the difference in accorded rank, inner power, and actual pride, made for a master/servant relationship, and they could ill afford going separate ways. In fact, with their titular changes, they elected—in the manner of vampires seeking closure—to change their names. Angruin would become Drac—Count Drac, the dragon count. Fangli, long used to the language of the north, decided to name himself Lókestámo, for bereft of noble title he felt that at least he could bathe in his master's glory— even a shadow can be feared. Henceforth he would build up his reputation as the dragon helper. However, the dragon shape had now been claimed by Necuratu, and reclaiming it would face his wrath. Besides, to use it again would annoy the Great Council. So for the time the Count shelved the idea of acting as an independent dragon—except perhaps where no witnesses would survive to tell the tale.

As for acting under allegiance, on the one hand, the Count's heart was more fully at one with the Necros. On the other hand, the Count's pride forbade him to return to Necuratu as a mere count, though he would doubtless have received rich rewards. Forcing himself to forget his own folly, he was minded to blame the Children for his undoing.

They had besieged the Dark Lord, who seeking release had stolen his dragon shape and created a dragon from beasts of Usen. That had attacked the besiegers, and Elaran had blamed and banished the wrong dragon. Damn the Children! His hitherto playfulness veered now towards unhealthy hatred. He sought to slay, not simply to play. And Lókestámo, what choice had he?

Thus together they ventured into the kingdoms of the Children, at times spreading dissention through their wiles, at times slaying for slaying's sake, leaving a surreal trail of bloodless bodies, yet always the trail went cold. And why should it not, when by flight they could escape the ablest hunter from among the Children? But as Count Drac became more comfortable with the Necros, Lókestámo became more uncomfortable with the Necros—slowly, ever so slowly. Even so, for Ages they journeyed side by side, while Middle-earth slowly changed. For over time Necuratu was banished into the Void, and his lieutenant soon followed. The firstborn would yield up their dominance to, and become estranged from, the secondborn. And long a dynasty of the secondborn endured, until in the plan of Usen the chief thrones of the Philikoi were removed, allowing the Dark King to turn Arda into a silent planet, severed from the Cosmic Powers of the other worlds. But the Dark One was limited in what he might do, having to ask of Usen himself for actions beyond his remit. It has been told how Usen, harbouring no evil nature, nevertheless used Necuratu to sound out his Children, to winnow them as wheat, bringing forth a great good through, and to the despite of, the Evil One himself.

Evil oft mars evil, it is said. The firstborn had for the most part left the shores of Middle-earth, whether for the immortal lands or for other mortal lands. For the most part, those who remained in Arda faded in mind, in body, and in significance. Yet in the will of Usen a hidden few bowed not the knee to infirmity, but rather grew in the knowledge of Usen, aloof awhile from the secondborn, and they learnt by prophetic word that by the Fire of Surtur they would reunite.

Of the secondborn, after the blessed kingdom of the Fourth Age ended, there arose war between mighty kingdoms, and none kept what they called their own. Weapons of mass destruction were devised, noxious fumes that poisoned the very air, and Arda became darkened. Interpersonal relationships shared in the madness, as marriage died and diseases ran rampant until death did them part.

Such evil was ever the working of the will of Necuratu, gladdening the Necros. That time of madness was ended by an explosion from the pits of Arda, covering the earth with a ginormous gaseous cloud of deep darkness, shutting out the light of day, and with freezing winds causing cataclysmic die-off. At last some few, some very few survivors of the secondborn, struggled back to the Vale of Sleep—though they remembered it not—where, it is said, within the Arboreal Temple, Usen himself reaffirmed marriage.

Since the Great Cloud, the millennia had simply flown by, and the Count remained in glorious isolation. He prided himself overmuch, and that made facing his weakness worse, for he could hardly deny that he was weakened. The fact that now he often reminisced when his body slept, reliving his glory days, told him that his life was now ikabod, a shadow of its original strength and splendour. He tried to suppress that truth, yet he could at least glory in revenge. He who had done no wrong had been wronged—or so he said.

In spite of injustice, he, Count Drac, had helped mankind to the verge of total disintegration. No doubt the Great Council was jealous of his perspicacity, but again, what thanks did he get? Mutually assured destruction had been all but certain, man abolishing man. Now that would have been a real smack in the face for Usen. Yes, yes, Necuratu had played some part too. And of course, mankind itself, having a bent towards rebellion, autonomy, had played its part manfully. But he fancied the idea that his part had been the most significant.

For him it had been a bold policy, for his own food supply might have been cut off. But then it had after all been based on the premise that his people were enslaved in their own minds by the Eighth Law. He had reasoned that if suddenly cut off from food, they would of necessity rise as one body, summon all their remaining strength, and defy Usen to do his worst. While dying was a horrible prospect, the chance of him escaping from this miserable planet had at that time made dying a chance worth taking. Yes, he had risked their lives—all because he wasn't enjoying life—and expected their praise as if he were the solipsist of dark dreams!

Ah, but to fly free once more in deep heaven—perhaps escaping to a far off galaxy—to feast again on cosmic rays—having cast off their mortal bodies—that would be revival. From a platform of almost pure frustration, it had certainly seemed to him a good idea at the time, and wouldn't have done his prospects any harm either. Vampires were community creatures, and even in deep heaven would have formed a flotilla needing an admiral. He had ventured to hope that for releasing his people from their fear of death, they would dissolve the Great Council, and depose Nindara in favour of him. Toba had disrupted his plans. Man had slowly clawed back from the brink of extinction, putting past factions aside.

But again, he had stepped in, and this time neither humanity nor Necuratu could take any credit whatsoever. If Usen had interfered to stop his plan for total annihilation of the Children, perhaps he could, without Usen's interference, affect their total subjugation? In his mind he had Ages ago conceived the nephilim, and that time he had not shared that thought with any other creature, awaiting its ripening. Dragons had all but disappeared from the Earth. Some had been slain along with their control spirits, usually dunamoi but more and more mere diaboloi, who were as rider to steed. Some 'steeds' had carried on riderless, such as lava dragons, or the Swat River monster. Some had been slain, whether by Guardians, as was Orochi by Susanoo, or by warriors of the Children, such as Georgius from Cappadocia, or had even repented, such as Tarasque, tamed by a mere woman—and a fat lot of good that did him! But long before that time dragons had become deregulated into all shapes and sizes—and at least one, Lagarfljót, actually preferred iced water to lava lakes, bidding fire-breathing begone. The dragon era had all but ended; survivors had mainly gone to earth—or under it. Spawn of a spirit enslaved! But he, the Dragon Count, would outlive them all. Yes, he had heard that Necuratu had made the same boast, but he was more copy-cat than dragon-king, an ancient and slippery snake who should be seized and bound yet again. Another thousand years in the Void might cool his breath! Necuratu had never been for the vampires, but the Count had.

Alas for the nephilim. Usen had had a hand in their destruction, aided by the vampire king, Nindara. If the king had had more sense, he would have backed the war, would have stepped aside and let the Count take the throne, toppling the Great Council. Indeed he the Count had long prepared for such an overthrow, and secretly built up hopes among likeminded discontents, giving them expectations of forming a new Great Council under King Drac the Devious. But the nephilim had been a realistic chance of a brave new world, if only the Night Kingdom had supported the venture. The Count was not to blame. Usen himself would not have dared gainsay the vampires in solidarity, and had only counterattacked knowing that divided they would fall. Then Nindara had stuck the final knife in, and twisted. That was sad for Count Drac to reflect on, but no sadder than for others, but for them the Count neither bothered nor understood: the Count was for the Count only.

∞

In days few now remember, the ancient *Sefer Bereshit* spoke of the heavens as having been created on the second day. Some, pondering those words, wondered whether the nephilim had been created that day before the living history of Earth began. They had a point, some shred of truth, but say rather that the Simbolinians, created in deep heaven before Earth's history, far into its history fathered the nephilim, though as fathers were not of nephilim kind. Somewhat similarly, a jackass might father a mule—does that make the father a mule? Say also that the nephilim dimly captured the light of their spirit-fathers, somewhat as the dragon race had weakly captured the will and might of the diaboloi. Ah, but weep, weep for mankind that the nephilim were ever brought to birth, yet weep not for man alone.

Tauresgal had stood alone in the great wood. Alone he stands thoughtfully, for he has a secret tryst with a woman of another race, a woman once known as Rátek. Ránpalan his father would have called him a fool, for her race were evil. Though now recognised by the firstborn as distinct from the diaboloi, nevertheless they were decidedly dark, deadly, and dangerous. Lore about vampires had slowly evolved. Memories went back to elder days before the sun years, when vampires had first toyed with the blood of the firstborn. That, it seemed, was all but a distant memory, but had become a common concern among the secondborn. The sindeldi, the remnants of the firstborn, had come to realise that vampires simply found the stakes too serious to attack them. Off the hit list, their gain was man's loss, man being a soft target. Even so the sindeldi were wary, for vampires were consummate stalkers of blood. Besides, vampires had been known to enslave the secondborn, giving themselves eyes and ears among those people. Who was to say whether there were slave-spies within the sindeldi? Yet Tauresgal's heart had been moved by his converse with the vampire lady. He trusted her. Trust is of course an intangible mystery, and like love is sometimes misplaced, yet those who have it not are the more misplaced. An imperfect science, trust is personal, and to trust is to be vulnerable, but to be mistrusting can be depersonalising, so deadly to the soul that you might as well be in your coffin. He, being an imagodei, chose to trust her, based not on her beauty but on her words, her demeanour.

The first encounter had been strange, for he had come upon her lost and languishing in the woods. She had been wounded and was weak, wandering even to death's door, and divining her type his instinct had been to dispatch her with all expeditiousness, with as little compunction as swatting a mosquito. Her eyes had expressed her melancholy expectation of her end, and her hated helplessness. He had hesitated, and as many a time is seen, they who hesitate are lost. Yet perhaps having been lost, he had found a thing of rare beauty. He looked on the outward form, and was deeply moved. He looked into her heart, and was profoundly stirred. For sindeldi too are telepathic, though generally of lesser degree that vampires. And although vampires commonly shield their hearts from their own kind, towards this sindeldi lord her shields had been down in her despair. And he had spared her, even tending her wounds. More vitally, he had given her shelter and protection, while she healed her body through her own thelodynamic power.

For her part, she had been touched that a natural enemy, her natural though forbidden prey, had shown actual kindness. Nor had he sought to capitalise on her vulnerability. He could have imprisoned her to gain information or other advantage over her kingdom, but he had made himself vulnerable to her. And when she was hungry, her enemy actually fed her. Not with the body of a secondborn—for they were sacrosanct—but with the blood of animals—for they were not. When she thanked him, yet confessing some need for better blood, he had actually bared his neck, obtaining first her word that she would not drain him unto death or dominion. He had believed her, she his enemy! Her heart was strangely warmed towards this sindeldi prince. For many weeks they had communed together, opening hearts and minds. He had in all honesty openly sided with the Guardian who had defeated her in the skies, whom in pride she had sought to bring low. And she, she had been tempted to side with the Guardian too, for her defeat had brought her great gain.

Soon she was healed, and returned to her own people. Of her meeting she kept quiet: to play with food was considered unwise; to praise living food was considered damnable and deadly devilishment. To reveal it would be to endanger both Tauresgal and herself. But she had made arrangements to meet him again in those dark and deep woods, either at the wolf moon or at the snow moon. Now wrapped in the forest mists she glided silently down, morphing into her humanoid shape in his presence. "Greetings, my lord Tauresgal. I Kiskilla am returned, and would speak more with thee."

"My Lady Kiskilla, I am come alone and unwatched", he replied. That neck of the woods was seldom walked by his kind, being the land of the Oldest Couple, Powers sent into the world before the Shaping Wars. Their part had ended Ages ago, but still they dwelt in Middle-earth, though had moved once or twice. They messed with none, nor were messed with by any. *They*, it is said, yet they had long become as one, and were content with each other as with themselves. Masters of none by none mastered, free. They claimed neither land nor river, yet the very earth claimed them, delighting to honour them. Tauresgal had been in that woodland to visit them, not for counsel, not for anything but their company, a delight afforded to only a privileged few of the sindeldi race. And though they did not watch, they would be aware, affording Kiskilla space to be renewed. That itself convinced Tauresgal that there was good in her which could triumph over evil. They had walked on, at first with the quiet contentment of friends, but after some time had spoken of deep things, things which Kiskilla had puzzled over.

From their talk, she came to see that the mercy he had shown came from the imagodei, the clear radiance of Usen within creation. And beyond the mere mercy of forbearance, he had given of himself, of his own lifeblood, and that with a trust which vampires were strangers to, a trust that extended beyond the borders of kind. And all this, he claimed, was of the very nature of Usen. And it tasted good, yet was a forbidden fruit. It was a heresy, but a rich heresy. True, she remained an enemy of Usen, and he would slay her as soon as look at her, but at least she was not an enemy of one of his children. "Do you not risk your life, my friend, in befriending me? Might it not be that Usen will hear of this, and punish you in the fire lake?" Tauresgal had laughed cheerfully at the idea, saying that he had Usen's smile. There he could not be right, for her people knew Usen better than did the sindeldi, even though the sindeldi were among the Children—for in longevity they were but as children to the vampire race. Still, he trusted Usen better than she did, and this idea, trust, was seductive. It was like the idea, peace, when your whole life is lived in constant fear—seductively sweet but too risky to swallow. They who put down their sword will die by the sword. They who pick up trust will die betrayed. And yet...

Under the watchful yet carefree eyes of the Couple of Wood and Water, Kiskilla and Tauresgal began to meet with each new moon—snow, worm, pink, flower—and throughout their many names as now are named. It was not many moons before Kiskilla's greeting had become "Greetings, my love Tauresgal", or before they walked hand in hand throughout the green woods, where none would disturb their disturbing affection. Nor many more before their love became conjugal love, the highest of mortal loves, the giving of the one to the other, and the other to the one, the two becoming one in mutual slavery. Nor many more before her people knew of that union.

Yet to them she dared not call it love. To them it was generally tolerated, a mere itch which Usen's children could scratch. Between an interspecies couple, a bit of a fling without affection was socially acceptable—for most. Of those who countenanced such union, opinions varied as to whether any offspring should be terminated—whether before, during, or after birth, was immaterial—but at least it was agreed vampires should never bond with their offspring. Yet Kiskilla violated both taboos. She deeply loved her husband, and likewise her daughter, Lona. It was perhaps the seed of her redemption—yet none must ever know. Her husband of course knew, but his lips were sealed by wisdom. But her daughter, well, her daughter grew up without knowing her mother's love. It had to be so, for both their sakes, lest the Night mete out death to both. An unguarded word could let the dangerous cat out of the bag.

Only to Nindara had she attempted to sow a seed of doubt into the hard-baked Night soil. Only he could have changed the law. Although vampires shift shape according to their will, their chosen default DNA is humanoid. Since it was a rule of their order that they never committed to vulnerability, they never committed to each other, and their family camps were based purely on family fiction. They tended to eschew husband/wife links, but enjoyed father/mother links among their own kind. They would not have wished DNA links between themselves, even had they been able to procreate Pneumata, but Pneumata could not give birth to Pneumata.

So the only unions of interest were those between them and lesser creatures, the Psuchai, the Children of Usen, towards whom dominance and convenience were the keywords. And most hybrids were as disposable as the unions. To Nindara she had quietly suggested, only suggested, that maybe, just maybe, Usen's children were not, well, not as Usen, that is, more like hybrids, perhaps worthy of respect in spite of their parentage. She could have made a stronger case, had she been both prepared to admit to love, and to explain how the enemy had befriended her in her hour of need. No, that secret had to be kept at all cost. Nindara simply was not prepared to hear. "Fool, hurt-but-hate-not is our motto, but would you have it to be love-and-hurt-not? The Children are not to blame for their father's sin, yet their father must pay, and since he will not pay directly we can but extract payment from his children. Thus they are our lawful prey, minding that the firstborn are the more dangerous to play with. It is pain, not blame, pain moderated according to our need to survive, a need Usen has caused, so must pay by the blood of his own. What good does it do to disassociate the Children, who must remain our food? And why respect them anymore than you respect the grass on which you tread, the clouds over which you fly? Foolishness! Let me hear no more of it, on pain of my great displeasure." She doubted herself, doubted her love, its very propriety. Yet one fact remained, she loved her husband and child.

∞

Count Drac had had setbacks, but at last he deemed the time to be right. For long he had ventured quietly among the vampire nobility, flaunting in private his punishment of banishment, and seeking out allies from among the hardliners, those who felt that Nindara was too soft. At last he had enough power at his beck and call—one hundred and ninety nine, to be precise. Two hundred had long been deemed a fighting number. In default setting, each vampire had ten fingers.

Since unity is strength, let the lesson of ten fingers teach networking with another, yielding ten vampires as a team. And as a square is stronger than a line, so at the next level let ten was squared, yielding a hundred in strength. Greater strength needs greater coordination—from the lesson of the two hands, double the hundred, with one leader.

Together at his summons, they assembled in the Haunted Valley, a land between mountain ranges, which in the Third Age had been the throne of power of the Dark Lord's servant. That servant had never been more than the claw of Necuratu, when scratching this side of the Void, and had soon joined its fire-black master on the other side. Of course now its master was back, no longer playing with fortresses, but hiding intangibly in the shadows—hidden lord of the diaboloi—and the Land of Shadows was vacant for vampire incursion. The mountains of ash and of shadow had undergone both risings and fallings through seismic shifts, but were still held in veneration by the Necros and the Night. There the Count made his hidden headquarters.

Though trade from Poiana Slatinei in the east, made them just a teeny-weeny bit too salty, the local Kocofeni people there made rich pickings. Just as well, for the Count's band chose to conceal their operational base, so were restricted to local cuisine. A small contingent of the sindeldi king had also established a base in the mountains, concealed from man but hidden there to seek and destroy any risings of ancient evils, for rumours had unsettled King Ránpalan. Cleverly the Count had begun those rumours, the cat summoning the mice for a bit of mongrelising. His two aims had at last coincided: a healthy and hidden sindeldin population, and a healthy and hidden vampire population—mice and cats unknown to human kind.

Feeding so many hungry mouths, the human population soon realised that it was in some kind of catchment zone for nonhuman predators, things that went bump in the night. It began to wonder whether those who had died of unwed mothers, returned to seek blood vengeance on errant fathers, and whether the practice of painting such bodies in ochre would prevent the birth of bloodsuckers: what fools these mortals be! The artwork idea had surfaced numerous times over at least 40 kyr, possibly by sellers of ochre in vampire intensive regions. To compensate, vampires quietly helped protect the human population from human invaders, so death rates remained about normal for that time and place in man's evolution. The wolves did not wish their sheep scattered. Now came at last the time for the giants to be born, and for the world to weep.

SEVEN

Hopes Swept Away

At last the hope of Count Drac was in place. At last the hope of Kiskilla had come to pass. Kiskilla had a need, long unrealised, for bonded companionship, for two-way lifelong commitment of life to life, person to person. By free marriage she had found this freedom, and she had been fruitful and had multiplied. Not a vampire child, of course, since spirits did not give birth to kindred spirits, but a child of her husband's kind, an imagodei. Yet she knew that her inner fulfilment had to be kept under wraps, since it jeopardised her whole family: affection was heresy. Even Lona must grow up under the belief that her mother cared not for her. The only affection she found was among her father's kind. Political correctivism gains votes sure enough, but it can have a suffocating effect on the young and innocent who pay for those votes. But that's the way it had to be in vampire society. Under Nindara the sindeldi were simply food, not friends, despised children of Usen, to be sometimes tasted, generally tolerated, but neither tormented nor treasured. Elsewhere, also under wraps, the Count's hopes ran smooth to plan, and the fruit of his genius was beginning to bud.

Some say that channels of the Dark can masquerade as agents of the Light. Perhaps they have a point, but it had certainly been that the Count and his followers had masqueraded as sindeldi from Ránpalan, and that the Count had transformed his shape into that of Ránpalan's firstborn son. Appearing to the Carpathian community, their storyline was that the king had commanded there to be an Apuseni community, hidden in the western mountains, hidden even from the Carpathians. This would be the smaller, secret reserve, and maidens were required for its wellbeing. That was certainly different, yet the Carpathians had no reason to doubt the prince's word, and the Apuseni 'sindeldi'—though keeping aloof under Ránpalan's orders—had soon selected potential mates. It was most irregular, but the logic had been that after a few years the maidens would make their individual decisions as to whether to stay on—perhaps to marry—or to return to the Carpathians. Seemingly Ránpalan's urgent will, it was quickly obeyed.

Yet never was band of 200 maidens so saddened. For once safely away from safety, theirs was not the lot of freedom—choosing if and whom they would—but of bride-enslavement. True, that has been the unhappy lot of many before and has been since, yet their mates were not even of their own kind, not even the lesser children of Usen—such matches had been few though free and fruitful. No, theirs was the unhappiest of lots, for besides being enslaved to aliens, their very motherhood was alien. The one relief was that each had a settled mate and knew no other. No longer maidens, they who needed no medical assistance in dying sure needed it in giving birth, and it was a wonder that some survived and were able to heal their wounds.For those born were monstrous indeed. Their sires had manipulated their own DNA, experimenting, ever experimenting, without ethical safeguards. What cared they for their slave-wives? It was the will of the Count. The creatures that came forth came forth before term—of necessity. Well nursed, these hatchlings continued to grow, hideous and huge. The idea first conceived in the dreaded mind of Count Drac, had now been born through women of the sindeldi—the days of the nephilim had arrived to haunt the Children. Usen saw and was displeased, and the sun was darkened in the sky, disconcerting the Apuseni vampires.

"My master," said Lókestámo, "you have succeeded in provoking Usen himself—his displeasure is delightful but dangerous. You have also gained a gallant following from the Kingdom of Night, and conceived a Child army, the like of which has never been seen. Surely now we may break free from Nindara, and align with the Necros? Should we not dispatch therefore these spent mothers, draining them to the last drop?"

"My friend, do you fear their testimony against us, and that they might escape to endanger us? Let us bravely stand on the verge of this new era, wherein we need fear no more. Usen has fought against us for his children; now his sons by us shall fight against him—will he not back down? And they can enslave women of the human race, and so Usen shall have repugnant Children from the two races, Children mixed with our image, Children confused.

"With nephilim by sindeldi and giants by man, we can dominate his world to which he bound us, stirring his bitter cup in sweet revenge. Then will not Nindara bow the knee to me, and the Great Council beseech me to return as tyrant? Will not Necuratu himself envy me my ingenuity and surpassing greatness, and curry my favour? We shall be the head and not the tail. Yes, soon. *Apropos* these women, I had wondered whether to use them a second time, but by using their progeny we can glean sindeldi maidens without recourse to subterfuge. But to calm your fears, my friend, let us now to their deaths to end their woes, draining their blood in their death throes. They matter little to me. And let their sons join in the revel, baptising them into blood!"

And so at last the slave-mothers were released from their bondage to the chilling arms of the Dark. At last they welcomed the warming arms of death. At the fathers' will, their unnatural offspring joined in the slaughter, old beyond their years were they, and indifferent towards they who had birthed them. For affection was of no value to the Dark. And perhaps the slaughter helped to calm hidden fears within the Count, fears awoken from slumber by the pertinent advice of Lókestámo, fears still denied.

Their two hundred sons were mighty, biological distortions of great size, and combined something of the telekinetic powers of vampires with the youthfulness of sindeldi. Able to blend in with the very rocks and hills, they outsized all living things on Earth, and the will of their fathers controlled them. And something of the dragon fire of the Count had gone into their making, thus it was that they had a heart of fire that could sometimes be seen through the joints of their rock-hard hides. For a time they lay imprisoned in the Apuseni Mountains, and their food was harvested from the humans of the valley, brought to them in their seclusion. They could rest long without food. And rest they did, other than in mating with human women who were brought in with their food. Female offspring were simply killed without mercy either before or after birth—in its evil the Dark valued not unborn women. Such fathers cared not for their babies, nor were they of their own kind anyway. Nor cared they for their melancholy mates. Thus arose a race of lesser giants, the elioud, under the will of their nephilim sires, even as the nephilim were under the will of their vampire sires. Let those who cared for Usen care for their children, if they willed—the races of the Dark cared not.

Soon these creatures closed off the valley, and the Count again appeared to the Carpathian colony—well before the 2 years was up.

He spoke a supposedly secret message from Nindara, to up stakes and walk the ancient roads to the Iron Mountains, and to wait ensconced. His wording precluded any messenger returning to Nindara—fact checking would expose the lie. The Count had long ago studied Nindara's heir, and donned a perfect ghost-likeness. Thus sindeldi protection was removed from the secondborn, allowing Count Drac's new army to quietly mature, fed on the creatures of the valley of blood, helpless before the grim reapers. They were as those trapped within a cave, with inexorable hands reaching in to grab whomever and whenever at will. The womenfolk served in one way, and the menfolk in another. None were wasted, and Count Drac hugged himself. Only after the valley was drained of its Kocofeni people, did his glutted army arise in might.

His malicious eyes turned to Land of Two Rivers: revolution must begin somewhere, and where better than at the heart? At first he led his people due south for the Wadj-Ur, always travelling at night. Vampire scouts ensured their secrecy, so that they were not heralded before their time. From Wadj-Ur they hugged the shoreline, heading east but curving with the coast south as needed—except for inland diversions to sneak past places like the fortified city of Ugarit—going by the valley route to the east until they arrived at a tall mountain range that looked west towards the sea. And there on that ice-capped peak they held their last council. Count Drac the stirrer sat aloof, letting his people have their say, smiling to himself. "We go now to war," said Shemjaza, "and we may multiply, but only from the human women. Inanna has promised herself to me alone, that we may begin a royal race. Therefore, any who seek to molest her I shall destroy, but of the rest, have your fill." Inanna would have been highly incensed to have heard that, but Count Drac, who loved her not, had fed him that lie. With the eyes of imagination he had foreseen a time when his army should be turned against some of his own kind, those who sought neither Dawn nor Necros and were content with the Night. Bitter disappointment could flow from resentment to strengthen his hand at time of need.

"Think rather that this is neither raid for women nor for new race, but war to dominate the Children; to darken the light of Usen. Any who are not discriminatory shall die. To the men of Darkness, freedom; to the men of Light, slavery. Who then shall seek slavery and oppose us? Those of the darkness shall be useful tools in our hands. Would we destroy useful tools? Spare not simply the women, but willing and unwilling slave-men. Thus shall we build our army", said Azazel. "As for Inanna, count her not your own, Shemjaza, but let her judge between us, if she be truly of the Dark. Otherwise, let her be destroyed beneath our heel as undark."

"What of Usen? Will he not oppose the darkening of his image?" asked Uzza. "Are we not safest to abide in these hills, only at need venturing further afield?"

In exasperation Shemjaza retorted: "I fear that you fear, mighty though you be. Put fears aside! Usen has betrayed his own weakness, for he has allowed us to be created, corrupting his image already. He has stood back while we wiped the blood of the Kocofeni from the Haunted Valley. Has he not shown that he fears to oppose those who bear his image? If he dare to dissent and dabbles in our affairs, I shall take the brunt of his weak-willed wrath. I fear him not! Come, we stand on the verge of the Nephilim Years. Do not fall in fear! Swear now that we shall all stand and play our part, and that the hand that holds back shall be hacked off." Thus he sought to bully into his ideology.

Thus spake Azazel: "Yea truly, we go in Darkness unto Darkness, for it is a holy war against Usen. The lesser Children shall be baptised into death, darkness, and despair. Between the rivers their men shall craft weapons new—blood shall be their sport. Their women will veil themselves in vanity and deck themselves in disease, caring neither for marriage nor for children, but for the fleeting moments of meaninglessness. Those of the Light shall fall under their oppression, suffering alienation by their *gattungswesen*, their very inhumanity. But the Dark shall wrap themselves in witchcraft, and Usen shall weep and repent."

All this the Count saw and smiled upon. These were useful servants, able to take command of themselves. Too dismissive of Usen, no doubt. But then he encouraged their delightful pride in the Dark. Little did he foresee that after their rampage would come a rainbow, gracing the world with a reawakening of righteous relationships in the wake of disorientation and confusion. Usen was watching, giving time for his own to turn to him in submission—what had they to be proud about? Slow was his nature to intervene in the affairs of his own creation, but his days would be days of renown—to bless or to curse. These things Count Drac knew not, for his mind was blinded by fury and folly, he of a darkened race. From the mountain they arose in great grandeur and glory, taking the path due east towards the rising sun.

∞

The black headed people cried out is panic, as they beheld the Count's army wading in from the north-west. To them it was if mighty údugs had descended from the skies. But whether in war or in peace, none waited to find out. Shouts and cries echoed through the towns and villages. Some ran to the temples. Priests prayed purposefully. It was all in vain, for Count Drac came in war unstoppable. Here, in the land of Nindara, he sought to make his first statement—and first impressions count. Here he made war against Usen's children, not against his fellow vampires. The people of Ránpalan were at first involved, but as an isolated force. The sindeldi had long been sundered from man, and deemed it perilous to seek out mortal man, ever prone to betrayal. Yet as older to younger siblings, they sought to befriend them at times, while guarding their true identities—they were legend. Now as on the QT they roamed the land in small groups, walking with arms concealed. Ránpalan was not a skulking king to hide within his cave all year long. He too was out. Often in the warmth of summer they slept out hidden within the trees. Much they had suffered at the hands of Necuratu and Count Drac. Much more they would suffer—was it the will of their father?

The blood-red blush of dawn flushed auspiciously for invasion, a warning to those shepherds that watched their flocks. Sindeldi had walked the woods in the heat of the night, and were now encamped on the verge of the forest, looking onto the fields white unto harvest. Some humans, making an early start in the fields, paused to wonder about the storm cloud brewing on the western horizon—a dust storm, perhaps? The dark cloud seemed to be sweeping swiftly towards them, like giant trees wading with the wind, wrapped in coal-black cloaks, an incoming tide of life or of death. From the cover of the green woods the eyes of the sindeldi king saw not trees, but an army of giants ploughing through the land, and soon through the farmers.

He stood watching in amaze, frozen to the green turf. This monstrous incursion was a one-sided affair, for what use were scythes and sickles against such hideous hides? Yet the slaughter seemed not indiscriminate, for for the most part the giants seemed to ignore the younger womenfolk, and a few of the men were brushed aside. The watchers of the wood watched aghast at this terrible new menace. To the quickness of their eyes and minds it seemed possible that the men who seemed only concerned with their own skins, were the ones most likely to keep them. To the sindeldi, such pitiful lives should least be kept, for the sindeldi were naturally protectors and connected naturally with those of like mind. Was a race fit to live, if only its least fit to live lived? Care for others is the cohesion of community, and without such there was no community, simply unconnected individuals—inglorious isolation. Most communities could survive carrying a few such individuals, could accommodate them—but enough reflection, the incoming wave had to be stemmed. Ránpalan threw caution to the winds, and at his battle cry his people sped from the woods, weapons unsheathed, shining in the sunlight.

Sindeldi swords were of ancient make and metal, bound together with skills beyond the lot of man. Had the giants found their match? Into the thick flew Ránpalan, Torodagnir slashing. Many a giant was dismayed by the speed of the sindeldi and their swords, which caused pain but killed them not. Others were pained by quiverfulls of arrows that pierced their eyes, but blinded them not. The giants were slower but unstoppable, a giant wave surging over the unprotected land. The most that the sindeldi could do was to distract them, allowing the humans to flee.

To the eyes of the giants, the sindeldi were as grasshoppers, nay, as nasty gnats—annoying but not annihilatory. And without further help, what could they achieve except to put off the inevitable? But still they stayed, some spending their lives to buy the lives of Adam's children. But too few, all too few.

From a nearby hill fort, a lookout witnessed the battle. He cried out that ekimmu from the woods were engaging an army of fallen údugs—did the ghosts seek to be freed into peace, for fighting the údugs to save man? Whatever, it looked like they needed help—couldn't údugs be killed by mortal man, even if the ekimmu hadn't a ghost of a chance? Swift thinking Shesh-kalla, ugula of the fort, quickly calculated the fight. If they joined the ekimmu, together they might defeat the giant údugs. However, if they stood back and the ekimmu were defeated, the údugs might then pick them off easily enough. Thus it was that he threw his men into the fray.

Soon men and sindeldi were fighting shoulder to shoulder against the nephilim army, and seemingly making some headway. For the giants were confused by the numbers of creatures swarming around them, and swung their clubs clumsily around them in frustration. It was far easier when your enemy fled from you. But while many strokes went wild, some found their mark. Of the smarter giants, Shemjaza and Azazel ignored the vermin swarming at their feet, seeking to espy who was in command.

Thus it was that soon Ránpalan was seen to lead, and Tauresgal was identified as his personal bodyguard. Thus it was that Shemjaza and Azazel came against Ránpalan, mindless of the rest of the rabble. Although cumbersome, the tree clubs descended in tandem on Ránpalan, who barely managed to dodge them. "My father," cried Tauresgal, "now danger is concerted towards you, the fight is unfair. Flee my lord, and I shall hold these giants at bay."

Again both clubs sought out to strike out the light of Ránpalan. One he dodged, the other Tauresgal deflected with a shield. "Tauresgal, these giants must be fought, for otherwise they will surely sweep through this land unchallenged. We must not give way." Again the clubs swung, this time felling the king. Had it not been for the swiftness and braveness of his elder son, he would have been crushed under the stone boot of Azazel. Upholding the king, Tauresgal quickly wove through the mêlée, with Shemjaza and Azazel lumbering in hot pursuit, pushing aside friends and foes alike. King and prince alike turned to face the foe. Torodagnir flamed blood red, even as the first traces of the yellow sky fought to outmaster the red dawn. Against Shemjaza the king lunged, piercing deeply the mortal hide. In pain the nephil cried out, first of the nephilim to know such searing pain. But one sword, no matter how mighty nor by whose hand wielded, could not slay the two hundred.

A new sword arose at his side, for Shesh-kalla had also seen that Ránpalan seemed to be the leader of his people—"Shesh-kalla for the ekimmu!" he cried. His sword was good, but was no more than the biting of a gnat. Shemjaza was not dull enough to the pain of annoyance, nor wise enough to ignore what could do him no harm. It was impertinence, and must not go unanswered. Thus he turned with baleful eyes upon this son of Adam. Azazel too turned from Ránpalan, misled by following Shemjaza. Oh how different might man's future have been, had Ránpalan been slain on that field of battle! But it was not to be. "My liege, we must flee this fight. I hear this word from Usen!" declared Tauresgal, a noted visionary. Ránpalan was a wise enough king to make up his own mind, and that dictated that this fight was for fighting not fleeing. However, he was wiser in heeding Usen's words of wisdom. Had not Usen sent a distraction, allowing him to escape having bloodied his foe? Had he not learned wisdom about their future fate? Now was not a good day to die, and so without further ado he turned and darted away, disengaging his people.

To the Black-heads, it was as if the ghosts of man had man forsaken— beyond doubt ghosts could die, for they were departing in haste! As the sindeldi fled the scene, one departed not. Tauresgal knew Usen's voice, knew that to stay was certain death, yet before him stood Shesh-kalla of the fort, who had come to their aid. True, had the fort not come to the nephilim, the nephilim would have come to the fort. Yet Shesh-kalla had not risked battle in that certainty, but to save those he believed to be divine ghosts standing by man. Should not at least one such 'ghost' stand by him, the brave defending the brave? Perhaps Tauresgal also divined an important future for the line of Shesh-kalla. However that might have been, what is known was that as Shesh-kalla had distracted the mind of the nephilim lords, so now Tauresgal did. His sword also was of ancient craft—though not as potent as the dwarf blade—and this time Azazel was deeply cut, though not so deeply. Yet his cry of anguish was the second which went up from the nephilim that day.

Telepathically Tauresgal commanded his extricating people to snatch Shesh-kalla away from the fray, while he commanded the attention of the giant leaders. Yet that meant both that he could not for the moment dodge towards Shesh-kalla, and that his own defence was fast disappearing—mere men could not defend him. Pretty soon he stumbled under a blow, for others had now turned on him. Few of the Children still stood, and many lay dying on the field of trampled emmer wheat. He too lay as a Child with them, dying as did they. As his life fled from his body he remembered the warning from his wife, not to involve with the lesser Children. Yet he in honour had followed his king into battle, and in honour had forsaken his king to save he who had saved the king. Somehow both had been Usen's will, and it was a good death. Yet "farewell sweet wife and daughter. May we meet again." And his sun set in the crimson field.

As the light of day withdrew for that night, the Count and Lókestámo strolled through the wreck of battle. A day of triumph and of smiles. The sindeldi had met their forces for a brief skirmish, and quickly withdrawn hopelessly outmastered, a spent force. The humans had almost divided themselves, and the Count flying high above for reconnaissance, had soon adjusted his instructions. The Children who scurried slowly away, were most likely to be the older women, or those carrying their young. Those who sped away, were likely to be the selfish women and the selfish men. Hah, they run all away, and cry, 'the devil take the hindmost'! So be it! These who sped the quickest were of some valuable to the Count. The slower should be slain, along with those who held their ground. That would save interrogation time—they did not require all the evil men, nor all the women, and they could always check out the captured men at leisure.

Although he and his 199 vampire followers had a telepathic hand on the 200 nephilim—who in turn had hands on their lesser offspring— they were otherwise free to herd their booty safely away from the battle. Darkened Children were better than deceased Children, in the Count's eyes. The towns of Rapiqurn, Zimbir, Kazallu, Neribtum, Tutub, and cornered Eshnunna, had all been defeated in the blundering blitzkrieg. Some food had escaped southeast along the valley towards the gulf—the Count had been flattered to let fear flow forth across the nation.

Well within a week the country would be Count Drac's in entirety. Already Zimbir, bird city of the king of the Black-heads, had fallen. The women wouldn't be wasted but would be put to good use. The men would be segregated into Light or Dark, lest any righteous remain free to undermine the Darkness. For the chosen few, some women were set-aside for their use, their entertainment, their diversion. Covenant bonding was outlawed, divorce made mandatory among the lower classes. After all, marriage was anathema to the Night—it offended the sensibilities of the Dark. It was strange that rumours would soon begin to fly that these nephilim were údugs, Powers fallen because they had fallen for human women. Necuratu shook his head in wonder at human folly. Fallen aggeloi were disgusted with the very idea of being enamoured with creatures of dust—and not even of star dust! The Count was bothered neither by rumours nor by human timescales, for his mind worked in millennia rather than in minutes, and he counted his life in the billions. When his borders were secure with stock locally born and bred, he would look to break out of these repressive borders. Sorting out global humanity would take some time, so let it be for now.

Within some years a new generation of giants had been conceived. Once more the Count saw that among human females, few mothers remained fit for reuse as secundigravidas. Theirs was not a happy life. Happier were those allowed to conceive and to raise normal boys and girls into adulthood, repeatedly providing replacement stock. That was according to nature. Following the initial domination, the virtuous could be allowed to live under watchful eyes, acceptable if for no other reason than the sport of the Darkness. Dull are the cats that lack mice. Mice could be useful; and why fear a bee that has no sting? Quite rightly only a few rose into the ranks of virtue, since humans were now raised in the relationship of vice. When tempests their warfare are waging, when the elements madly around them are raging, who dares to be different? And—once nature lacked the modelling of virtue—ill-nurture often triumphed over normal nature. Among that silent minority, even a talented few got posted into the lower positions of authority, yet always under the warning eye of the

Black Force. Teasing them with a little authority inculcated impotent rage—delightfully amusing. They couldn't stray far with such puny powers, but were offered more power by knuckling under. After a while, vampire eyes didn't need to be so watchful anyway, since evil men had taken over the dull task as thought police, conforming law into evil. The Count himself wondered how far virtue would go with the odds stacked against it—curiosity would not kill the Count. Take away their freedom of expression, take away their livelihood, will they not curse the failed creator? Take away their wellbeing, would they not damn him, stick a spear into his very side? How that would warm the heart of Darkness!

The next king chose to forget the former times: Zimbir had become an unspoken memory of pre-conquest days. In mockery he maintained that the kingship had now been lowered from heaven to his city of Shuruppag. By that he meant that his dark masters were the true masters of heaven, taunting the Faithful that while virtue didn't pay, vice paid dividends: the old heavens seemed as dead as a dodo. The king's men didn't experience the problems common to common folk; they weren't afflicted as lesser mortals. They wore pride as necklaces, every morning putting on violence. Their eyes bulged from obesity, and their imaginations lived in the land of sin. They were mockingly malicious, arrogantly authoritarian. They rejected heaven and claimed the earth. Best join them and be a treader, not a trodden: yet in the Dark, Light holds its own. Their giant masters encamped in the surrounding high places, where the chosen mothers to be, lived in a central herd. The more fortunate women were simply set aside for evil men, scattered throughout the land—fair game for the taking. The cosmic orientation of Ubaratutu, Shuruppag's king, was evil. Had Usen been more patient, Ubaratutu might have reigned much longer than his 31 years. Usen rarely got involved in any big way, but when he did he was a game-changer. He was dangerous, sure, but like a lion, usually safely ignored. Of more concern was the lurking reality of the sindeldi. And even closer to home was Light corrupting the Black-heads. "Ziudsudra my son," asked the king, "how goes your mission?"

"Ubaratutu, my father, it goes well. Those of the Faithful are under our fist. The Confessing still seek the customs of older times—of marriage and the bearing and raising of children, pshaw! And likewise of heart homage to the Oppressors—whom they call Guardians! Breaking them from these things goes well, however. On those who renounce them, we bestow career enhancements at our right hand. On those who do not, we punish with a heavy left hand. Many have converted to our new ways, but some few remain bigots to the ways of Light, refusing to see the glorious Dark."

"That is good, that is very good", opined his father, signalling his son to depart. At an early stage Ziudsudra had been brought to the attention of Ubaratutu, as a brilliant young man well skilled in the art of control. He had taken a fancy to him, and before long adopted him as an only son. And as his son—who his real sons were he neither knew nor cared—he seemed so far to have exceeded all expectation. Many of the Faithful—a.k.a. the Confessing Community—had been obstructionists to the new society, and had been hard to deal with. Ubaratutu would have had less of a headache had he simply been allowed to butcher all that opposed the Dark. But for some unaccountable reason the Count had issued orders to spare their necks though not their backs. As a matter of fact, Count Drac had wished to stretch righteousness beyond breaking point, for the broken were more entertaining and educational. But many had gone underground, and when on the surface were disguised in the masks of Darkness. That made it harder for the State to discriminate the good citizens from those of the Light. With Ziudsudra as his son, Ubaratutu found that the pure of the land were being better identified and silenced. Perhaps the Count's experimentation would go well after all. The king had soon made his son king over the priesthood, commissioned to teach the arts of deception, witchcraft, and sin.

The temples had been raised to the divinities, places to contemplate their attributes of Light, to sacrifice to them, to evoke them and to be—like them—pleasing and acceptable to Usen their high king. But now the temples were places to indoctrinate the people into new ways, disloyal to and displeasing to the divinities. As priest-king, Ziudsudra did the rounds, ensuring that the priests proclaimed the spirit of the age, not the spirit beyond all ages. Or so it seemed. In reality, Ziudsudra worked under Guardian Enki and was an istar—

indeed he was nicknamed Atrahasis, the exceedingly wise one. Masking himself as an agent of evil, he was in fact a Guardian, turning surveillance, target acquisition, and reconnaissance, into useful intel. The Guardians had been caught off guard by the Count's bold plan. Interference with the Children had always been a softly softly thing, and usually spiritual warfare was only provoked when diaboloi got too pushy. Here a mashup of the Children had joined the game, altering the dynamics. Ziudsudra's body was expendable as he worked among the Dark. His plan had been to quickly gain the trust of the king, obtaining a position of influence. To those of darkened minds he spoke Darkness, but if safety allowed he spoke Light to those of the Light. He played a dangerous game. Telepathically linked to the Guardian Kingdom, he fed intel and tapped into their minds. Drastic methods were being considered. Should there be total extermination of the Children? Should there be some survivors to repopulate the land, reviving the best of the culture?

Working under orders, first Ziudsudra leaked the rumour that Anu and Enlil were deliberating on whether to drown all the Black-heads—even the royal and priestly. Second, he secretly recruited Noach, a trusted woodsmith of the slaves of Sihon, to build a boat. Noach, relocating to the backwaters beyond Shuruppag, got on with things, and Ziudsudra secretly supplied him with the necessary finances, and also with witnesses as to his madness, so that neither the nephilim nor their guests would get wind of a serious rescue mission. Nearer the time, aggeloi would lead sand and sky Phusika into the giant sarcophagus-like monument—called *Coffin to Life*. There they—a male and female of every basic kind—would be safe, ready to reproduce and diversify. Of those that had evolved according to the kosher norm, an extra six pairs for six days of celebratory sacrifice. For when the voyage was over, Usen's children would come out, expressing their cosmic orientation in proper respect and gratitude. In line with its name it would be like a giant elongated coffin, ten times as long as it was high. Onlookers might think that it was a symbolic work of art, as if housing the three nephilim leaders—or did it symbolise their doom? But as the hired carpenters said, there were three decks—a bit of a squash for the nephilim lords! Rumours of Noach's madness—reinforced by his preaching at them—kept the project a purely local jest.

In pretend concern Ziudsudra bowed before Ubaratutu. "My king, it is rumoured that the Guardians plan to wipe out our entire people, killing even the nephilim by an epic flood. At your command I shall build us a giant cube, a life preserver for us along with our masters and mistresses."

"I too have heard such surely specious rumours, my son. I have dismissed them, though they trouble my people. Yet I see our advantage in such fears", replied the king. "Very well, build some floating cubes. Spread the word that we will only allow rescue for the best of the Dark. Let the Guardians be besmirched. Publicly proclaim that our noisy parties have disturbed their precious slumbers. This way, we appease and displease the masses. As for me, I will feign repentance to the Light, and in writing urge you to encourage a moral *volte-face*."

"My lord, why risk that? If our masters dethrone you as a rebel, our subjects might revolt! Would you tarnish your good name?" enquired Ziudsudra, concern written all over his face.

"My son," replied his crafty father, "my dark master will forgive my sin, for by it I will take King Ránpalan down before we drown—if drown we must. Subterfuge is needed to draw him from his secret lair into our lap. Don't you see? Believing that we are turning from the Dark, he will come to our rescue and be caught, and seeing his blood run will warm my heart."

And so it was that, capitalising on the public fears about a mythic flood, the king issued advice. He did not use his royal-person name, Ubaratutu—the way he issued command from his throne. Rather, he used his royal-city name, Curuppag, as if his city was his beloved son—the way he issued advice from his heart. So as Curuppag did he write unto his son, Ziudsudra, advising virtue, and failing not to honour Guardian Nisaba, she who blessed their grain and inspired writings of wisdom. He advised that men should not buy prostitutes—they bit back; and that prayer brought abundance, like cool water cooling hot hearts. Many more aphorisms and pithy maxims did he write, which were circulated around the kingdom, to Eridu, to Lagash, to Nippur, and to Tutub, and to other chief places, all bait to catch Ránpalan. The Gutiums—neighbouring nomads—

would spread the word further afield. Closer to home, Ngushur, as chief slave, must be deceived, and must secretly sell the fake news to Ránpalan, until the trap was sprung. Ubaratutu had certainly been giving it some thought.

And so it was that Ránpalan, ever prepared to risk life and liberty in the pursuit of virtue, left the safety of his secret caves to liaise with Ngushur, undisputed chief of slaves. It was decided that acting as a covert go-between, Ngushur would set up a meeting king to king, in the lower valley between Larak and Nippur. And so the next battle was set up. For it is a matter of primeval protohistory, that as menacing storm clouds gathered, in good faith and hope Ránpalan set out seemingly with but a small guard. Yet Ubaratutu had had Ngushur followed, though only as far as the mountains, and his return path, issuing forth to the valley, had been marked. Thus had Count Drac been informed, for both servant and master had an interest in the death of the sindeldi king. And the Count had ordered Lókestámo to waylay and slay Ránpalan. Lókestámo therefore had set up an ambuscade at the feet of the hills, with reserve strength within the valley, springing the trap as soon as Ránpalan passed the ambuscade.

Leading a small number of lesser giants, Lókestámo sprang towards his ancient enemy, trapped between his force preventing flight into the hills, and reinforcements that prevented flight into the valley. And yet Ránpalan had prepared for some such trick. He had had reinforcements shadow his small band, and so Lókestámo in turn found himself trapped between Ránpalan and Ránpalan's reserves. Fiercely they fought, energy bolts of dark light from the vampire leader; ponderous clubs from the giants. Lókestámo took out many of the sindeldi by his energy bolts, yet his power was not unlimited. Each bolt drained him, and not every bolt found its billet. In fact his bolts were not wasteful but mild, intended to wound, not to kill. The sindeldi was quick, often able to avoid his bolts, but if stunned by bolts they became prone to the slower clubs of the giants.

For their part the sindeldi used speed, sword, and shaft. Darting around as if playing tag, they ran rings around their foes, firing arrows into them, and leaping in with pointed sword. Their arrows infuriated the giants, thus reducing their fighting abilities, and their swords did damage. These lesser giants—and Lókestámo had unwisely taken only a small force for better concealment—were more pervious to harm, and although needing many wounds to be slain, were eventually taken down, though at the cost of Ránpalan's entire company, so even had been the match. Lókestámo himself had been wounded by blade and arrow, the swiftness of the sindeldi at times having proved too much for the energy shielding he had raised in his defence. Out of the blue sprang Shesh-kalla, who had been among those shadowing the king, but had watched from cover. Now that he thought that his sword could count, he sided with the king, setting sword laughably against Lókestámo. The brazen effrontery dumbfounded the vampire lord. Did this creature of dust imagine that he could endure even one energy bolt? Yet its very audacity moved his heart, as was seldom moved. Deflecting a thrust from Ránpalan, Lókestámo quickly disarmed Shesh-kalla, and held sword to throat. And Ránpalan hesitated.

"Sindeldi king, I am wounded and weak, yet you stay lest I slay this man? It is not as my people would do. Strange are your ways, yet long have I pondered, I who am but a slave to my master in the hope of princedom. Yet if my master is to gain flood instead of land, has he not failed, and if failed, will he ever become king and I become prince? And yet as prince would my soul be satisfied? You, who are master to this mere man, do lower sword that I should spare him, yet my master would not seek to spare my life. Let us stay this fight." With that Lókestámo released Shesh-kalla, that brave fool who had risked life that the king might live.

"Lókestámo, once my people looked down on the secondborn of Usen, divining not their devotion. Behold Shesh-kalla, usenic of heart, and ask whether the path of virtue is not the better path", urged Ránpalan.

"Long I have apprehensively asked of virtue—but would it welcome me? To break with my dark lord is surely to break with my dark people. Yet my troubling thoughts have been sliding unstoppably away, for the Light offers a glorious generosity of spirit that moves me unasked. Long has my heart hounded me to surrender in gainful defeat. Behold, I place myself at your feet. What penance must I perform?" asked Lókestámo, suddenly kneeling with the hilts of his sword downward before him.

As Ránpalan sought inner wisdom, the word of Usen came unto him. Unto Lókestámo he answered: "That you change your name. Be no longer Lókestámo, dragon-helper of ages past, but be you Alessandro, man-helper of the age that is and is to come. And to confirm your repentance, I shall commit my faith in you unto you, that being on trust you return never unto wicked ways. Behold, I make you custodian of my sword Torodagnir, Troll Bane in the language of man. Preserve it, that the line of Shesh-kalla—to whom it shall belong—ends not, for I divine that it has a mighty part to play. Now I see with the eyes of Usen that Count Drac will never rest content until you and this man are as sheep before his wolves. Therefore for your safety and for your penance, go swiftly and silently with Shesh-kalla into the far northwest, even unto the land of the midnight sun, that land of snow and of ice and of misty mountains that now border the great sea, even to Gundabad, where the high king of the Adopted awoke in ages past. Long there shall you guard his line, even mayhap until the Fire of Surtur—for which I see now that I too must await, though in seclusion, a hidden unknown to disturb the Dark Mind, and a trump card to be played in the final game. Yet in that ancient land Torodagnir shall play its part, for many trolls have gone to ground there, such that even Guardians might dread."

With some sadness, yet with some satisfaction in being entrusted with Torodagnir, Alessandro—who had been Lókestámo, who had been Fangli and many names of Dark before—prepared to depart in long sought peace. With him, now thoroughly soaked to the skin, stood Shesh-kalla, a man with a high and lonely destiny. As for Ránpalan, his heart warned him that this rain would clean the valley of the nephilim, but would endanger even the high ground, and that his northwesterly halls must be sealed against rain and ruption.

Together they would journey northwest for a while, Alessandro, Nindara, and Shesh-kalla; vampire, sindel, and human. The rains were beginning to pool. Ngushur, having been warned in a dream not to return to Ubaratutu, had smuggled away as many of his fellow slaves as he could gather together on short notice. So it was that before Nindara turned for his home within the Khurrite Kingdom, he met the contingent of self-emancipated Black-heads, and divined that it was the will of Usen. Taking swift counsel among themselves, they therefore all began a swift flight to his mountainside abode.

Meanwhile in Shuruppag the rains were beating on the houses, rata-tat-tat, as if to summon the people out. Well, a wee bit of wet on the neck was nothing to write home about, and the land was used to warm and wet weather. That the clouds boded ill was admittedly unsettling, and admittedly some citizens were on edge—after some nasty rumours had circulated. However, hadn't the king made reassuring noises to mollify Enlil, and so avert the wrath of the divinities? Still, the clouds looked like clouds of vengeance to many, and staying indoors might be safest. Besides, the king had had some giant cubes built, it was said, and had contingency plans to rescue the best of his subjects at a pinch, hadn't he? If things really did look black, he'd promised to call and collect them, if they proved faithful. So yes, stay indoors for now. And there were also hills one could go to if the rivers flooded—sailing was a breeze on a fine summer's day, though not so brill in a storm.

"Ziudsudra," demanded Ubaratutu, "where has that dog Ngushur gotten to? He took slaves to bring back logs for your confounded cubes, but word has it that the guards have had neither sight nor sound of him these ten days, though search has been made. You should have supervised them better, and I shall flay them alive if I get my hands on them. I am wroth, for word now has it that far from here some fool named Noach has been inciting discontent among my people, calling imprecations upon my name. What kind of man is he that is so brash? A madman, as some say? Is he one of ours who has gone bad, building some sarcophagus for our masters? He must be arrested and executed, I think."

"True my lord," replied Ziudsudra in contrition, "such a fool must die, but I fear that his comeuppance must be staved off for a while. In this downpour, even walking without has become slippery to the sole. Once the rains have eased never fear, that woodsmith will be here. As for the cubes, alas, without the extra timber so far only two have been built, which I have named *Preserver of Life*, and *Enthroned over Water*. The former is but basic, the labour of but few days, but many weeks have gone into your majesty's cube, and even Enki of Eridu could not build a better. But surely neither Enlil nor Anu his father, will sweep away the wicked with the righteous? Besides, have we not deceived them by your exhortations?"

"Maybe we have, and maybe we haven't", grumbled Ubaratutu. "If the Light hears that Lord Lókestámo has sought to destroy Ránpalan, then they might disbelieve my show of repentance. The Guardians can be deceived, but should not be underestimated. I sit uneasy until he returns, for he is the viceroy of Count Drac, who commands the giants. With him we will surely be safe."

But Lókestámo did not return, and the rains did not cease, and King Ubaratutu simmered in impotent rage. With the persistent rains, the rivers arose and overflowed their banks. Many waded in the new riverlets that coursed between their houses. There were farm animals to be looked after or brought to the slaughter. Some even dared to offer some sacrifices to the Guardians, but the only hearts they offered were animal hearts, and their prayers went unheeded. Some waited for the emergency plans to kick in; some, crying *sada emedu!* sought out higher ground, implicitly showing divergence from their king. But then, why bother catching rats that desert a sinking ship? Let the rats sink wherever they fled, and let mud be their grave.

It was not just the humans who were suffering. The nephilim were struggling to stay afloat. Scaling the heights was easy when firm and dry, but when water washed over hills, and even mountain tops were but extra heights to slide from, well! For the most part they sheltered on ledges, hunkering down during the storm. Giant numbers had greatly increased since the days of their incursion, as had the Count's hopes for world dominance. He had counted on Usen being unwilling to destroy those who bore his own likeness. Had Usen decided that enough was enough, and commanded Enlil to flood the nation? Or was it merely a parochial plan of Enlil's? If so, Usen might countermand Enlil's order, but if not the order could be fatal to the Count's plot. But either way, the Count was helpless, his hope of becoming king fast draining away. Lókestámo had sought out the life of Ránpalan, and the Count awaited at least some good news on that front, but his servant was outside the range of his telepathy for now.

Meanwhile the *Coffin to Life* was being slowly floated by the waters. All sorts of non-predatory animals were on board—their fear of man had deflated while their fear of the sky had inflated. Some Phusika even had prophets—often mere runts—seers that could dream dreams and see visions. And they came in pairs, male and female, but to say that they came as husbands and wives, or were monogamous or polygamous, would be to confuse the Phusika (who merely mate) with the Psuchai (who marry)—romanticist and risible rubbish. Noach had invited many of his people to the grand opening, but all knew that he was off his rocker, didn't they? Alas, the wisdom of the Phusika was wiser than the wisdom of man! And apart from Noach's immediate family—a slave seldom knew extended family—only Phusika had tickets to life within that great wooden coffin. The first mega-tsunami that struck was as massive as it was unexpected, and the water overwhelmed the people like an army that rushed on a city, that ran upon its walls, that scaled houses and swarmed through windows like thieves. Surrounding homes were more than flooded— they were ripped apart.

Debris—animal, vegetable, and mineral—was soon floating past Noach's *belem*. Built alongside a mighty river, the belem was soon violently buffeted between the outgoing and incoming currents, but the workmanship held good. It had been doubly waterproofed, too. The main door had been shut and sealed by the site foreman, known locally as Puzuramurri—later believed to have been Ninagal himself—just before the rains had started. They would have to endure a long and patient wait, before it would be time to disembark and to reintroduce species back into their native land. From the perspective of Noach, days and nights blended into one, and the seasons seemed to pass by without respite. Long they felt that they were even floating over the surrounding foothills. Well, the waters must be mind-bogglingly deep, since almost half the height of the ark was well under water. Whether or not the hills still rose above the waters was academic, since with such torrential downpour not letting up for weeks on end, no creatures could even survive on flooded islands. Even if they could cling on to trees, without food they could not cling on to life, and weakened would have been washed away. The view was nothing to write home about—indeed, home was long gone. For from under the eaves of the roof, they saw at most heavy mists which would long hide even high mountains from sight. Perhaps they were floating between mountain ranges through flooded valleys and gorges. If so, they were being steered by watchful aggeloi helmsmen, for never once did they encounter any obstruction. Where they would land was an awaiting wonder.

∞

As to the cubes of Ziudsudra, consternation awaited the king. For as the rains showed no sign of abating, and the rivers showed signs of flooding, the royal household reluctantly realised that their world might be totally engulfed, and they boarded the royal cube. Well it had been adorned with rich tapestry, even down to ornate boxwood eleven-stringed lapis lazuli lyres (one thirteen-stringed), plus drums, rattles, and cymbals, for all-in onboard entertainment. Royal musicians, singers, and dancers, had been kept in preparedness in case of evacuation. Dried foods there were, along with flagons of water and of wine, and favourite morsels for the king's household. Decks there were, and ornate bedchambers. Ubaratutu was accustomed to a life of luxury—why else be king? Following the orders of Ziudsudra, much fresh food had been resupplied daily, so that should the emergency arise with the waters, much fresh food would start their confinement. Goats milk, pig, deer, beans, barley, leeks, lettuce—you name it, they had it if it was to be had and was worth having.

And as they arose above the flood water, their anchors held. Of course, not even Enlil could create enough rain to overflow their floating *belem*, could he? They had not counted on tsunami after tsunami, however. Nor had they counted on betrayal. The royal cube had been whitewashed, and had looked shiny and new. But though externally a work of art—and internally palatial—Ziudsudra had purposely side-tracked the builders from basic waterproofing. In short, the cube leaked big time and was going nowhere but down. Soon it would be full within of dead bones, filthy and slimy. The belem would resound to the clamour of bedlam, as slowly the trapped attempted to escape upwards, until there was no upwards left. As *Enthroned over Water* sunk under the waters, so ended the kingship.

The *Preserver of Life* was of different stuff. It looked rudimentary rather than royal, but it could float and its anchors could be ditched at need. Into this cube had gone Ziudsudra, along with his wife. It was so dark inside that not even the light of glorious Utu could enter, and though he was not often worshipped he was always welcomed. Having ventured in on a fine summer's day, Ubaratutu had vowed never to darken its dingy doors again—precisely what Ziudsudra had planned. As for he and his wife, they had the light of Utu within, and needed no sun. Their subterfuge ended, they could return to the Guardian Kingdom of Anu. Cubes aren't designed to be steered, and the huge cube was tossed about on the great waters, but the thelodynamics of Guardian Ziudsudra himself kept them level and moving through the storm unto the blessed harbour, a spirit portal or gateway, where the Guardian Kingdom intersected with Earth. They were borne upon the great Buranuna River which went forth into the Gulf and unto a land famed for the sun's rising, even unto a hidden hill of salvation in the sacred land of Dilmun. The name of that mount is sometimes said to be as far west and north, as it was said to be east and south, for it was hidden from the minds of mere mortals. Such rifts were more common in ages past, where the aggeloi or divinities entered or departed our dimension, usually in secretive places. In top-down talk you could perhaps picture them as ladders. Afterwards, some said that Ziudsudra had taken family with him, doubtless confusing his story with Noach's, for Ziudsudra and his wife were of the Powers, hidden, for encloaked in human dress—and had no mortal offspring.

"Hail, Ziudsudra and Shubanna, now mortalised", said Enlil, as the two Powers stepped from their cube to a right royal welcome.

"Hail, Enlil", they replied, bowing low. For Enlil, and his brother Enki, had appointed them for the task of going among the mortals as themselves mortal, incarnated, and to operate under deep cover they had become inextricably bound to those frames. Mortal death would cast their spirits beyond the confines of Anu's kingdom, into the bliss of the blessèd beyond, yet their hearts were still yoked with Arda.

Wise Enlil had long foreseen how parting would be sweet sorrow to them, and had obtained the grace of Usen for them to remain in Arda with immortalised bodies. "Glorious Ziudsudra, for long you shall be known as *Utnapishtim*, for you foresaw life beyond the flood, and *Atrahasis*, for foreseeing you then acted with exceeding wisdom. Your spouse and you have been faithful to your call and to your charges, for though much has been lost, much has been saved, seed-life to replenish Land of Two Rivers. The blessing of Anu therefore rests upon you both, and although your bodies have been prone to age, immortalised they shall be, by grace of the Guardians whom you have so sincerely served. Here upon this hidden hill you shall long dwell, seeing with eyes immortal the splendour of the land you have saved, and hearing of its joys. For under Ngushur a new kingdom shall arise, and shall for a season be blessed. He, who has fled with the sindeldi king, shall return with the righteous, and even the beasts from the belem of Noach shall flourish under the blessings of Anu, and multiply safely to live again in this land, which shall once more worship Usen himself through devotion to his humble servants. Under Ngushur, sky, land, and water, shall be blessed, for a while. For the Count's nephilim have all but perished, and the Night itself shall bring the errant Count to book. It is the will of Usen. I, Enlil, have spoken."

Many years later, Gilgamesh, mighty king of Uruk, met with Utnapishtim and his wife Shubanna, at one of the ancient portals of the Powers, and heard told the story of the Great Deluge. Though alas, with the passing of time and tongues, that story has come to be told somewhat amiss, yet even so it remains a mighty story of the glory and the wrath of the Philikoi under Usen, purging the land of those which would have enslaved all mankind. Of Noach, it is told that he and his family, riding out the storm, were swept north and west between high mountains, finally coming to safe haven. Of the Phusika within, all went well. Without carnivores to feed, basic dry fodder served for most. In charge of supplies, Emzara and the other women had planted many plants on the top deck, where watering posed least problems.

Noach had not been given to understand how long the voyage would last—Ziudsudra tended to be terse. But he had expected it to be long. The rains and tsunami surges had seemed to go on a generation of days, and it had seemed an interminable age before signs of dry land appeared. Heavy rain, intermittent rain, finally no rain, and clear summer skies burning off the water, baking the mud, Anu receiving back from Enki and restoring Enlil's land. At last Noach disembarked, giving thanks unto Usen under a radiant rainbow arching sky, a sign, Noach believed, that the nephilim menace would never resurface, and that the light of Land of Two Rivers would never again be snuffed out. Not alone would they return to the land, for Ránpalan had espied their landing, and had gone forth with Ngushur and his people to greet them. As was befitting, for six days they remained there, for six days sacrificing Phusika in toast of Usen, and feasting on them, whereupon they rested on the seventh before departing.

Ránpalan would not go with them, for it was the will of Usen that he lay dormant, aloof from man until the Fire of Surtur. Together, Noach and Ngushur herded the Phusika back into Land of Two Rivers, even unto the place of Kish, where many were released into the wild—no snake, scorpion, hyena, lion, nor dog or wolf, remained to savage them. And planting was done to re-establish agriculture. Indeed, one of the first things Noach did back in the land was to make some party wine—that the land would once more be merry. And it needed it, for the stresses and strains of the journey there and back were showing themselves in strained relationships. Noach rowed with a son, and a grandson upped stakes and headed off to the Great Sea in the far west, taking many of the Black-heads with him. Yes, a few party drinks drowned out the old pains, but they sadly caused a bag of new ones.

The Count had lost most of his nephilim. After fighting rough, Usen had spoken tough to King Nindara. Although banished, the Count had been caught and brought before the court. Lókestámo had been searched for, but had disappeared without trace, though no psychic resonance of any silent scream had been found in air or in earth. Not that it mattered much, for he had merely been the puppet, not the puppet master. But if Lókestámo was skulking somewhere, why, he would get it in the neck when unearthed, and punishment was merely put off.

"Count Drac," said Nindara quietly, "our enemy has come to me— following your folly—disturbing my dreams. Though he has unjustly bound us to this world, yet he permits us much freedom within it, even to the taking of his children, as he permits the Phusika of the carnivore kind. All this he reminded me. Yet he said that exceeding his patience you imperilled the global reign of the Children, by a monstrous race not of his design, combining both celestial and terrestrial from evil heart and with evil hands.

"He spoke of watching and waiting, wishing you would recant of your evil ways, or at least that his children would risk life for liberty, and rise above your tyranny. Few he found worthy to save, and in great sadness unleashed flood to revert his land to an earlier state, effacing your madness. It will be rebuilt, he has said, yet he shall now doom us, lest we vampires dare to so defy him again.

"Behold, the monster-children of your design have for the most part perished by flood, and their spirits which are evil shall be bound within the circles of this world until its end, bound impotent within the Kingdom of Necros, to which fate they belong at heart, though at last shall suffer the lot of the Children of the Dark, whether first or second born. Thus he has spoken.

"And thus I shall add: our people shall seek out any of the nephilim and their lesser brood that yet walk this world, and send them swiftly into death, that this world shall know only of their name. Thus we shall prove to our enemy that the Night repudiates the work of your hands, and forthwith stands aloof. May his heavy hand of wrath not come fully upon us, who already suffer confinement to this woebegotten world."

The Count feared for his life. "King Nindara, all I have done I have done for our people. We diminish; the Children increase, and will arise against us, unless we strike them down into servitude. Were that the Kingdom of Night aligned with the Kingdom of Necros, that Light would flee! How could I have known that the enemy would strike down those of his own children, holding us to blame? Knowing him as unjust but not as merciless, I was caught unawares, yet I meant well. But to what further doom will he put us?"

"Count, by Usen's *fiat* the infinitesimal waning of vampire power shall yield by steep decline to a mere tithe of what we are, lest we seek further hybridisation. For he knows that we must always be stronger than what we create—what slave creates their own master? Thus is my anger towards you, Count Drac, for by your thirst for your own glory—I see through your heart—you have stabbed our feet with a crippling blow. Think not in your folly that the throne of this kingdom can ever be yours, for unto your own people you have now committed the sin unforgiveable. Perhaps this time your life would be forfeit, should I take you before the Great Council. Seek its verdict if ye dare, else take that of this king. I sentence you to royal banishment by extraction. Among the unfallen vampires you shall find no friend. Only they of the banished shall be your friends—and they who are few shall despise you. My guards shall send you forth with scourging, who in temerity sought to overthrow me!"

Count Drac knew that the Great Council would not limit his punishment this time, and knew also that the king was not showing any great kindness by extreme banishment. What the fate of vampires was beyond death, they knew not. But within the confines of the body they shared the fate of their people. To live would be to suffer not merely the shared diminishing of vampire power, but the added pain that he was publicly blamed for it. Despised and rejected by his people he was of wounded pride. By extracting him from the kingdom, the king saved him from death, sparing him to suffer endless misery, as lowest of the low. The Council might mercifully put him out of his misery, but his fear of death outweighed his fear of living. So the Count did not contest the king, and fled as the king's guards pursued, lashing him with whips of thelodynamic power. Suffering shattered body and shattered illusions, sadly time was a healer but not a teacher, and he lived ever with hope of Nindara's demise—the royal exclusion would die with the king, defaulting to the Great Council's ruling, and perhaps reinstatement, perhaps enthronement?

The vampire king had punished, but not banished, the fathers of the nephilim. For in keeping them on his side, he had effectively banned them from helping the Count, since officially the Kingdom of Night was neither friend nor foe to those it banished. Superficially, the excommunicated called each other 'friends'. Yet such friends were egotists—and pride looks down in contempt, not up in respect. Such friends were in the same sinking ship, and didn't give a damn for their shipmates. The Count was cut off with none to help. Nindara hoped that his ex-brother wouldn't need help anyway. The Count had long been a walking disaster, too keen on the Kingdom of Necros for his own good. Yet the Count's mind was too committed to evil and to currying favour with the Dark Lord—hoping for reward—to dwell for long without planning new and interesting ways to inflict the Children.

The Black-heads' kingdom had resurfaced under the leadership of King Ngushur, who, having learned servanthood before the flood, became its servant-king after it. In Usen's will, the Black-heads had returned their allegiance to the Kingdom of Anu: the worship of Cosmic Powers of sun, moon, and stars—and of Kingdom Powers in the sky kingdom of Anu—was the litmus test of their underlying worship of Usen the Unseen. It would be many generations before he began a brand new training course with a brand new class, a class preparing the way for Hamashiach, a class antiquating the rough worship of the many. Until then, he humbly accepted kindergarten worship, for the people at large were not ready to learn greater lessons. After almost 300 years at Kish, kingship was given to the city of Unug, where there was the Anu Ziggurat with its imposing White Temple built on top, dedicated to the local patron divinity, Anu. Many of its secular were religious. Some probably had their heads too much in the clouds. For the priests that was expected, of course, and most of them felt that their work was enhanced by the zealous within their city, but many in the secular thought it remiss for their own ranks to get wrapped up in heavenly things, especially if they left earthly duties undone. By and large it was a happy and prosperous community, however, but the Count was stirring up mischief against the Black-heads yet again.

Beyond the high mountains lived a neighbouring, strange looking people, for these people were blond haired and blue eyed. They had been the dominant power, seemingly for generations beyond count even before the Black-heads came to the two rivers. It was said that the Blonde-heads had welcomed the Black-heads, ceded them fertile land in exchange for undying friendship, and taught them the worship of the local divinities. Ancient friendship days had given way to mistrust and misdeeds, for the incomers had themselves become a strong people, waxing while the Blonde-heads waned. Spiritually, too. The Kingdom Powers still maintained friendship with the Blonde-heads, the Arattans, as they called themselves, but a friendliness not as joyously returned as had been in millennia past. An evil influence seemed to be pervading that ancient people, putting them at odds with King Anu. The Philikoi grieved that their light diminished in that land, but little perceived the hand that diminished it. Until now the focus of blessing had been with the Arattans, but already such affection had been relocating to the Black-heads, who after the Great Flood praised the Philikoi for the Great Rescue—for the two had been one. King Mesh-kiang-gasher had reigned as a Child-son of Utu, who at that time had adopted the vampire Inanna—who would later be called Ishtar—to be a Spirit-sister. Vampires in good standing among the Kingdom of Night were to show no favours to the Children of Usen, but by allowing her temporary placement within the Kingdom of Anu, Nindara tacitly permitted her to bless with the blessings of Anu. Similarly, Lamaštu, a vampire placed with the Kingdom of Necuratu, was tacitly permitted to curse Usen's children. When in Rome—as people would later say.

Inanna had proven herself amenable to the Light—though Nindara assumed that that was superficial conversion. He assumed the same of Lamaštu, too. In both cases his assumptions proved false, but that is another story. How it would have proved had Inanna been attached to the Necros, and Lamaštu to the Light, perhaps only Usen knows. Would the curses of Inanna, and the blessing of Lamaštu, have been superficial, against their inner wills? Maybe. As it was, Inanna had proved her loyalty to Anu, her liege lord, and with her divine brother had blessed the Blonde-heads. Her own thelodynamic power was stellar, and she was cursed with an itch to dominate, even to exalt herself in the heavenlies, her waywardness being curbed gently by Anu as she climbed her ladder. She had enriched the reign of King Mesh-kiang-gasher, and in turn his son Enmerkar's reign, and being prone to a little pride, felt that she should be better acknowledged, even adored.

Spurning the Blonde-heads, to Enmerkar she turned to build her name, inspiring him to build temples both at Eridu, and unto Anu at Unug-Kulaba. Moreover she merged the Kulaba section of Unug with a section she glorified as her own, the Unug-Eanna district. Thus she exalted her name to the highest place, while affirming her loyalty to her chief and thumbing her nose at the Blonde-heads, though their royalty still maintained some gestures of loyalty. Indeed, at the behest of King Enmerkar, she authorised and empowered Unug to demand tribute as to a little brother, from King Ensukush-danna, lord of Aratta beyond the mountains of Susin and Anshan. Unug demanded precious metals and gemstones for a temple to Enki at Eridug. Failure to comply could put the Blonde-heads at variance with Enki. Thus it was that Luinim-gina, special messenger, was sent to King Ensukush-danna of Aratta.

"Hail Ensukush-danna, king of ancient people", said Luinim-gina, having bathed and anointed himself leisurely after his journey— though but a messenger, he brashly presented himself as an equal to this king. "Unug greets you. Behold, at the command of glorious Inanna, we are building a temple for the worship of Enki himself, he of the wisdom from many waters, whose knowledge flows through the rivers of life. It is at the demand of Inanna that you contribute to the glory of his temple, sending back with me those things that are written down in my list in your language and ours. Thus you will prove yourself a worthy worshipper of the holy údugs, and your realm and reign will be blessed."

"Luinim-gina, insolent mouth of Enmerkar, I believe not your words, that I should bow to an upstart of a people. Behold, Inanna is with me, her faithful servant, by whose hand I have been ordained as king and as big brother over the Black-heads, who now flourish where we graciously planted and watered them. Who are they who now demand tribute to their temples? Have we ever demanded their labour in the building of our temples? Could not my armies entrap yours as a spider does a fly? Though an emissary, your life is in the palm of my left hand. Beware your words."

"My lord king, I fear not for my life, for is not Inanna herself witness to my words? Beyond death I shall be with her, while you shall be tormented in the netherworld, if you touch her anointed. Moreover, without the blessings of Enki, drought shall waste your land. Will your people not rise against you and your house? If I perish, you perish, my lord. Use what wisdom you may have, and turn from your wicked ways in contrition."

"Bold mouth, I fear no man, but respect the Powers that be. That you build a temple to the honour of glorious Enki is worthy of praise, and to that end we will be happy to provide that which you have requested. However, be it known to you that we shall deliver as trade, not tribute, upon proof that you have spoken the truth about Inanna. My wise men will therefore weigh up your list, and compute its price in grain. Return to us with fair payment in grain, and you shall return from us with your list fulfilled. Speak further at risk of my wrath, but return in haste to your king with my words. May the Powers judge between us." The king arose, signalling his guards to remove the messenger from his court. And with unease Luinim-gina arose, questioning within himself whether Inanna had indeed turned her back on proud Ensukush-danna.

When King Enmerkar heard of the response, he too questioned whether Inanna had really spoken to him in a dream. Ensukush-danna, at the end of the day, was lord of a mighty army, and unless Inanna's favour had fallen from him, he would be unbeatable. Unless Inanna clearly spoke again, and spoke clearly of opposing King Ensukush-danna, then it seemed wisest to let things ride as Ensukush-danna had proposed: diplomacy is the art of compromise. To now call off the embellishments of Enki's temple, would bring down the anger of Enki, yet the only way to get such gems was from the lord of the Blonde-heads, and the only safe way to do that was by accepting the trade agreement. Inanna simply stood by and watched the saga unfold. She had more than once questioned the faithfulness of Aratta's proud king. He had committed his word as her servant to fair trade—would he honour her in that? King Enmerkar, meanwhile, had disappointed her by signs of unbelief. Perhaps he was not ready to be favoured by her.

To many priests of Aratta, Inanna had spoken in dreams and visions about her disquiet with the Blonde-heads, and about her new home in Unug. Yet a lone priest prophesied that Unug would be humbled by Inanna, and the voice of the one pleased the king more than the voice of the many. Moreover his chief advisor, Ansigaria, was bitterly opposed to the flea-ridden kingdom of Land of Two Rivers. When at last the grain arrived, though it came in good faith he refused fair payment. "What, am I an equal with your king, that such goods should be seen as barter? Behold, I claim this as tribute from my little brother, long overdue. All the more in recompense of your insolence. Begone, before I rip forth your lying tongue from your head, deceitful mouth, for have you not bribed my very priests to bear false witness for you? For behold, Ishkur of the Rain has blessed up with a bounteous harvest of wild wheat and of chickpeas, and what Ishkur has blessed has Inanna cursed? Nay, she still smiles upon us, and those who have lied of her shall feel her wrath."

Luinim-gina was downright disgusted by the fact that the Blonde-heads' king had betrayed his word. Could he not see that the blessing of rain was because of his promise? Could such a king keep Inanna's blessing? The more he doubted it, the less he doubted that Inanna had indeed moved to Unug. But how must he deal with this knavish king? Unasked an idea came into his head. "My lord king, is not Inanna the údug of war? Let she who blesses armies now bless a champion to fight on their behalf, as is more convenient than the effusion of much blood."

After deliberation, Ensukush-danna agreed with this proposal. Indeed in his pride he issued his personal threats to Enmerkar, claiming that he himself had issued the challenge. And Luinim-gina was content, knowing that counter-threats would be recorded by his lord, but that the contest would decide who it was whom Inanna favoured. No date had been set for this contest, and in secret the king of Aratta sent his champion to soften up the kingdom of the Black-heads. Someone had come to him from the subject city of Khamazi, a powerful sorcerer by the name of Urgiri-nuna, who had now swiftly departed for the city of Eresh, a near neighbour to Unug. Urgiri-nuna had his own agenda, for in years gone by he had had, and had lost, control of that people. Enmerkar was not his king, and he would gladly see him subverted, humiliated by the Blonde Head Kingdom. And Urgiri-nuna had real power of mind over matter, thelodynamism. When he had first heard of his king's predicament, he had decided to capitalise on the king's anger. Now, how could he sour things for the Black-heads? How could he be commissioned by the Blonde-heads? The king sought to send a champion! Well, he would be that champion, a champion of dark magic! And as to souring things, why, milk could be soured, and if he soured their milk supply the Black-heads would soon turn against Anu's Kingdom, self-isolating themselves from his blessings. That would make them ripe for a takeover. By his power he could introduce viruses from around the globe, and he knew of plagues that attacked cloven-hoofed animals, milk suppliers such as cows and goats. It was later said that he tried first to win over the animals, only cursing them once they refused to stop offering their output in honour of the local Guardians. In short, it was soon seen that his real beef had been with the Powers, not with the Phusika. Soon herds were as drying streams, sluggish, off their food, foaming at the mouth, suffering in their hoofs, piteously dropping their unborn. And the people wept, and cursed the údugs and their king who pretended that Inanna would protect them.

Urgiri-nuna laughed, but he was not to have it all his way. For cowherds and goatherds had spotted him moving suspiciously around the herds, and reported him to their chiefs, even unto Mash-gula and Ur-edina, true worshippers of Utu. Speedily does the spinning top on which we live spin, yet our sun races over 400 times the speedier around the Milky Way, and he who rides upon her is the Cosmic Utu of many names. Ah, well beyond the meagre mind of man is the tantalising thrill of the Cosmic Powers. The Earthly Utu is but a wraith of the Cosmic Utu who rides upon the sun. Ah, but what a wraith, able to see with the eyes of the sun-rider himself! His humble servants reported unto him what had been done in the dark, and he spoke with his Spirit-sister, even unto the vampire Inanna. And she, invited to intervene, quickly devised a plan. So it was that soon a strong sorceress apprehended and opposed the trouble maker Urgiri-nuna, even Saĝburu the wise woman. "Hail, Urgiri-nuna, champion of Ensukush-danna. In secret you have sneaked in among us, but in secret you may not leave. For behold, you must now pit your magic against my magic. Let us cast shapes, and let us fight one another through shapes, if you dare."

"As for daring," retorted Urgiri-nuna, "you shall see that my shapes are solid and strong, and I shall cast you into the great river Buranuna, witch." He had fought fights of magic before, when magicians had merely sought to impose images into his mind, trickery by hypnosis. They were simply not in his league, and he scorned this old crone who dared to challenge him. By the river they had met, and into the river he seemingly cast a substance like unto frog spawn, yet instantly from the river sprang a giant carp. For of nature he was a shapeshifter, and able to project from his own substance a physically separate—though psychically united—shape. Such a wonder should have overawed this mental magician, but lo, at a cast of her hand a giant eagle arose from the river, clutched the carp, and flew away. Urgiri-nuna trembled, for he realised that she must be of his own kind. This time he called forth a ewe and her lamb, for his shapes subsumed something of the nature of things, and the ewe would be empowered by a protective fierceness for her lamb. Might Saĝburu's will be weakened by her feminine call to protect offspring? But no, she saw through the sham and called forth a mighty wolf, which easily overcame both ewe and lamb. Thrice more did the champions employ their magic beyond this world, and thrice more did Saĝburu weaken her opponent. But to directly lock horns as two bulls, would risk the life of both, for she guessed that her foe was the Count whose reputation preceded him. No need, for losing the game of shapes was sufficient to banish him from the land.

Even as his defeat had been witnessed by soldiers of both sides—the Arattan bodyguard were disguised as traders—so must his apparent death be likewise witnessed, so as to make him unable to trouble the land again in that guise. Thus it was that Saĝburu spoke telepathically with Urgiri-nuna, concealing both her true identity and her guess at his, and offering him an acceptable way out. To show their real powers would be against the vampire code, bringing the wrath of the Night upon them. And neither were willing to endanger their cover-stories. *Vade ad victor spolia*! The Count must comply. Quickly they worked out their storyline. She would explain away his defeat by implying that she had had the home advantage, that the údugs of Eresh—Anu, Enlil, and Ninlil—had empowered her hands, she who might have lost elsewhere. He would admit defeat, pretend to beg for mercy, but be cast into the great river as if to drown. This time, well out of human sight, the shape of a bat arose from the river, and flew swiftly away. Once more he had failed, but to lose a battle is not always to lose a war.

Count Drac was a past master at playing one side off against another. Reshaping himself as Namena-tuma, advisor to Enmerkar the high king, he secretly visited the migrants from Aratta, tribute from their defeated king. In public cloaked, in private he conversed with their leaders, assuring them that in unity lay their strength. "Blend in with my people. Speak our language alone. Learn our ways with bricks and blessed *esir* for their bonding; unlearn your old ways with stones and slimes. If we see you as one with us, we will treat you as one of us. Yet there are some close to the king to whom my counsel and my whereabouts must be unknown." Thus it was that a few of the Arattans believed that Namena-tuma secretly spoke seed-thoughts among them, and without attribution his ideas grew among their people as weeds among the wheat, roots entwined. Yet for long the new wheat coming from the west seemed good to Enmerkar, for now the temple of Enki was bedecked in gems and adorned by gold—payment for grain given—and the slaves from Ensukush-danna, left largely to their own devices, were fitting in splendidly and seemed eager to begin a ziggurat of their own. Why should the king be sad, who had made it clear from the outset that he would punish misbehaviour by exile from both kingdoms, scattering malcontents around the barbarian lands and deserts, as just deserts? Clearly they had heard and heeded his harsh words, willing now to establish their good name within his kingdom, and to be at peace as one people—exceeding even his highest expectations. And a ziggurat temple would link them to the heavenly agents of Usen, giving them a common spirituality with the kingdom of Unug. Uniculturalism seemed to be the ticket to common life, at last speaking one language.

Yet under the cover of community compliance, the dark design of Count Drac was corroding its way in. For although at large the Blonde-heads knew Usen only through the mediation of Anu, it was the Count's plan to subvert even that dim knowledge, and thus to leave them with only the dark knowledge of the Dark Lord. Behind the scenes he had been exploiting the idea that Inanna had betrayed them, and that Ishkur had deceived them, and that therefore it was high time for them to deceive and betray the Guardians. Thus it came to pass that the ziggurat they built within Land of Two Rivers was not to the glory of the Guardians, but instead to the glory of Enmerkar, for—they were told in confidence—by diverting the Black-head king from the divinities, Inanna and the Powers would return to the Blonde-heads. Hoping for Enmerkar's overthrow and former times revived, they happily cooperated.

Job done, Enmerkar was duly flattered, and in pride sought to ascend to deep heaven above the Powers of Usen. And thus when the Powers of Light beheld Enmerkar, they grieved that his religion had become self-worship. For the Guardians knew the fragile heart of man, and that such folly from the great could undo the Two Rivers Kingdom, for pride was a thin edge of the wedge, and fallen pride could wedge a kingdom apart.

Already Enmerkar had begun to boast that his champion had humbled the king of the Blonde-heads, and that he himself was enthroned as the new údug to his people. For a coronation, a divinisation, had taken place atop of the ziggurat temple, where only a divinity should sleep or sit. And that it was people from the ancient kingdom that had done him such honour, seemed to assure him that divinity was his by divine right. That his fellow divinities did not show up to honour him, smelt of pure jealousy on their part, a stench to his nose. Ah well, they would come round, and if they didn't he could begin a new line of údugs. Already he had begun to make plans with the Arattan migrants, contemplating a united kingdom in tandem with Ensukush-danna, a united kingdom which could do what before had been impossible—undermining basic spirituality and enforcing a sterile secularism of splendid isolationism across the globe, even as a virus in one kingdom can lock down all kingdoms.

It was not to be. For the sake of the people, and acting under Usen, Enki stepped in. He stirred up his worshippers. Some he sent to form a swift alliance with the tribes to the south and west, bringing together a babble of many languages. Great rewards were they promised, and great rewards received. Some he sent among the Arattans themselves, warning all but their leaders to forgo the language of the Black-heads, to break the alliance, and to regain their own identity. Thus the Blonde-head community were divided and confused in counsel and speech, and many refused to work anymore on the ziggurat city of the Black-head king, mocker of the údugs. Such was their confusion of aims that great misunderstanding arose between the dwellers in Land of Two Rivers. And were the invaders from the south and west to be treated as friends or foes? And so King Enmerkar lost the chain of command, for he was fighting against the divinities, they were fighting against him, and his people and his slaves fought among themselves.

It was a careworn king who finally bowed his knee in the temple of Enki, before he who had divided the unity between the spiritually lax Arattans and the fallen Black-head king. There he received forgiveness. There he pledged that his crowning tribute, the slave host from Aratta, would be scattered, banished from host and home kingdoms, saving those who had heeded the words of Enki. The great ziggurat, the monument of his rebellion, would stand unattended, unmanned, and unloved, slowly fading into nothingness. Namena-tuma was questioned by the king and beaten with many rods, until it was settled that he himself had not gone among the people of Aratta. Saĝburu herself appeared at the seat of judgement. As the evidence was heard, she sighed a deep sigh, divining within herself from whence had sprung the root of bitterness. And soon after, the Great Council heard of the Count's mischief, which had led to Usen's intervention through his emissaries. Its fury knew no bounds, especially having shown leniency before to the bothersome Count. Though by royal decree he was already an untouchable unclean, law permitted the Great Council to intervene and punish in extreme cases, if a former subject was deemed hazardous. Count Drac was summoned for the last time unto council banishment. Sparing his life was no mercy, for to live was to be cut off in the land of the living, to live as one undied. And with one added twist: he would be entombed in deep sleep for millennia. It was a heavy doom, though history would witness to occasional jailbreaks, flirtations with freedom in his restlessness and transgression of set bounds.

ELEVEN

OBLIVITY

Count Drac had proved too hot to handle, and had been put on ice for millennia, by order of the Great Council. Then the Night enjoyed a time of peace and slumber. It was little enough corrective punishment, though completely justified. Would he awake from his deep sleep a sadder but wiser vampire? Even the most sanguine hope doubted that, but it was worth a try. Pride and greed stirred the hearts of the human race, many seduced by the Dark Side The world was slowly awakening to another boatload of big events, many based on power play—most spits and spats from a vampire perspective. Chariots of fire would soon wreak havoc both ends of the Fertile Crescent, wrong footing traditional warfare. The bobbing kingdom of the Black-heads had soon sunk for the last time—unsurprisingly. But surprisingly the kingdom of Nindara had sunk the sooner—he who should have outlived all human empires. For the Curse of Usen quickly infected the Kingdom of Night, and their inner power diminished. Some called it the Count's Curse!

King Nindara had not been impervious to this diminution—indeed he had been particularly prone. Already in the days of Šarrukēn—who established stability between the Black-heads and the peoples of the north—he had begun having senior moments. And when the kingship was taken from Unug to Urim—where mighty laws would be written in accordance with the true word of Utu (whom some now called Shamash)—Nindara had been fated to fall by frailty. His was the dotage death of one who too long had held the throne, betrayed by his impatient and irritated children. But truthless tongues tumbled into trouble, and with that fall, for the first time the vampires would have a woman to reign over them, even mighty Kiskilla—she who in the sindeldi days had been Rátek, and would become Lilith—she whose word was honour. And since with her rise to power the royal banishment by Nindara fell by the wayside, Count Drac—once brother to the once king—would have returned to the fold, but for his irrepressible itch for mischief. As it was, he slept on by the will of the Great Council, with rumours of the wakeful world weaving in and out of his sleep-ensnared mind.

∞

From the Yellow River People, warring clans united under flood-tamer Yu of Zhuanxu to form peace, forming through Qi, son of Yu, a small but significant seed-dynasty of what would become a mighty and proud nation. It knew something of the troubling influence of Jiangshi and his followers—lesser vampires than the Count, but still nasty little thorns in the side. It knew nothing of the sleeping dragon, however—he who might otherwise have joined with Jiangshi as an older brother. But the Count's legacy of mighty dragons still lived on, and was often engraved in art to ward off their evil. Yet in reaction to their great flood the Yellow River People turned inward on themselves for deliverance, and transferred their devotion from the Guardians to those who had lived and died before them. So much so that when Emperor Kongjia tried to reform their worship, dissatisfaction towards the Xia Dynasty rose like a wave. As it did again against the womanising and sottish emperor, Jie, whose advisor warned him, "Don't waste your life chasing after women! This has ruined many emperors. And though wine is for those who are in anguish, it is not for emperors!"

His advisor was summarily executed, and Jie mocked that the advice of any advisor whose advice got the advisor killed, was advice not worth taking: when vice reigns should virtue speak? Jie claimed the last laugh, but lost the Mandate of Heaven, and was banished by Tang of Shāng, and a new dynasty cycle arose. It too lasted around half a millennium, and it too failed under the depraved emperor Di Xin, who died at his own hand after bloody battle. Yet, coming from the loins of emperors, did not the plain and honest Kongqiu speak his silver words, that none should harm in ways they would not be harmed, so insisting that mankind was imagodei? Silver speech and smooth silk streamed from Shāng. Many more kingdoms would flow, but the Count was to miss them all, and of the romance of the Three Kingdoms—which lay on the other side of the cosmic divide—he would remain forever in the dark.

∞

Perhaps he did not miss out much from the land of dingoes, the land of dreamtimes, of *alcheringa*. It was a land that still remembered times when the Philikoi often walked undisturbed in silent meditation, a silent land where eternity could be clearly viewed, like a world between worlds. Of course it had not always been like that, but even with the ebb and flow of humanity the Guardians—even stormy Namarrgon—were still fairly laid back, though the Turannoi—like Thinan-malkia of evil name—were always present wherever man was, like flaming flies around the sweat of the scorching sun. A balance of power was maintained, so that the flies seldom bit. But even without diaboloi, what is human war? Is it not merely the aggravation of the normal human condition, needing only the human heart to explain it? Every now and again human tribes would arise in war against encroaching tribes, or encroach on other tribes, vying for food and water resources. Stone knives and axes were not only for felling animals or branches. And there were those there from the Count's people, but they followed their leader, Yarama-yhawho of the Head, and by and large partook of human blood only to slate their thirst. In short, they were generally passive, not aggressive; trappers of the night, not troublemakers of the day. They would not have welcomed the Count.

Even as stories had spread about the Philikoi being the ancestors of the local humans, so funny stories had spread about the vampires increasing in numbers by assimilating humans, but spirits do not give birth to spirits. They were from Simboliniad, and their numbers decreased globally, although they roamed—sometimes more, sometimes less—in any given area. Like crocodiles, they were not creatures for the Philikoi to deal with: both could prey on man; man could kill or live with both.

The land slept. Sometimes rapid bursts of incomers unsettled the landscape, and more blood was shed between haves and have-nots. And new ideas from the seas led to new artefacts, new animals, and different ideas about the noumenal, the unseen spiritual, as hitherto parochial perceptions rubbed together, sometimes sparking more heat than light. The sacred sites of some became the secular sites of others. Some despaired, and sailed from the land of peaceful beauty and of ghost gums, seeking islands afar. They who remained largely slumbered in their mind of stone and walkabouts. But more deeply did the Count slumber.

∞

Elsewhere lay a civilisation on the west of a great continent. There a white people—long remembered for their bushy beards and beautiful buildings—cut and engraved, using tools of iron from over wide waters. Cosmic history had been radically changed by a new mode of life—one from beyond the Dynamic Bubble had actually been born, shaking the kingdoms of Darkness to their very core. Rumours were spreading throughout the cosmos, yet the world stood largely unmoved, uninterested, and unaffected. Even so a seed had sprouted in a far land, and its shoot was beginning to stir, stirring desolate lands into freshness and fruitfulness. But far across an ocean to the south and west, the quake was not felt, not even the slightest tremor. There there still held sway the ancient courtesy of bowing in awe before the stars and the planets visible to human eyes, primeval knowledge that Cosmic Powers rode their orbs. These worshippers sought to record their world, no longer merely by mouth to ear, for they had invented a paper from the leaves of banana trees. Life was retold by the written word.

This creative people—like and yet unlike those before them—long delighted in gigantic landscape art, designs for the spirits of the sky to smile down upon and to bless. By removing the top layer of iron-oxide coated gravel, lines had been made between places of water, places where hermits of great wisdom dwelt and taught. Would the Powers not travel along these lines to visit and to bless? Priests lived in temple communes, dressed in ornate clothing which bore images of the divinities they stood for. Cloths from clothing of older times were mixed with more recent, and together were offered in death to the divinities, to link ancestors of the past with descendants from the present. Sociality was solidarity. These were a colourful people, largely left alone by the outside world, and doing very well thank you. That is not to say that their temples could not know flood and quake—but not all floods are by the will of Hashem the cloud-rider. It is not to say that they did not fall into evil. Indeed the Kingdom of Necros was ever at work, reshaping divine images from good into evil, and darkening minds. The Count would have stirred things up, but he stirred not.

∞

To the far north, though the cosmos had witnessed the changing of the guard, yet the Guardians of Asgard were still on active duty, awaiting their long stand down before the eschatological battle of the shrouded future. Torodagnir remained a terror to the trolls, yet for a time rested in the safekeeping of Guardian Odin. Those were turbulent days. Bonding with humanity, Odin himself had fathered a human child named Siggi. Siggi became a man of petty rage and of murder, but grew out of both, and his son Rerir had inherited his throne. Rerir's infertile queen, being of the inheritance line of Shesh-kalla, found favour with Guardian Frigg, and her prayer for fruitfulness was paranormally fulfilled. The Giantess Hljod, one of Odin's valkyrie, delivered to her a very apple of Idunna, curing and strengthening she who would be with child for six testing years, and would die to save her unborn, Völsung. At his birth her life left the land, and she was lifted up to the heavens to be a shieldmaiden. Völsung married Hljod (the Pneumata, being shapeshifters, could appear as fully human in size and frame). Thus in Völsung's line there flowed something of the spirit of a Kingdom Power and of a cosmic spirit, great warriors honed for the Day of Ragnarok. Life would often temper such souls with sore trials, for as gold is refined by fire and white heat, the best sometimes suffered most.

Other shapeshifters were also at work. Loki's rashness and roguery led to Odin being trapped by Hreidmarr, a dark vampire who demanded—for the loss of a son who had had a fetish for fish—a wergild in gold, which Loki had to find. Loki's 'finding' was by way of theft, and he stole the gold hoard of a dwarf named Andvari. Loki also seized from him a precious ring. That ring, housing the spirit of a dunamos, had enabled Andvari to shape shift in exchange for becoming Necuratu's eyes, ears, and voice, within Nidavellir. Moreover it carried the curse of gold, enslavement to greed, the bane of dragons. Evil divines evil, and divining its power Loki had tempted Guardian Odin with it, hoping to replace him as king of the æsir. Fortunately Odin possessed it merely moments before it moved to Hreidmarr, who became accursed.

Fafnir and Reginn, Hreidmarr's shapeshifting sons, were seduced by the ring and murdered him. Then they fell out: Reginn feared fratricide and sought a sword. When the time was ripe, Odin returned Torodagnir to Shesh-kalla's line, as a wedding gift when Signy, Völsung's daughter, wed the dastardly Goth king, Siggeir. Hers was an unhappy marriage, not least because Siggeir shamefully slew her father and eight of her brothers, feeding them to his werewolf mother. As the giver had come concealed, so the sword's true name was concealed, but as Gram or as Balmung would it be known, and dragon's blood it would drink. For Fafnir had taken shape as a deadly dragon to guard his gold.

His brother Reginn had offered his special skills as swordsmith to Danish king, Hialprek, and unto Reginn was given the guardianship over young Sigurd, son of Sigmund and step-nephew to the king— who had married Signy after Siggeir's unlamented death. And Reginn equipped Sigurd as a warrior, sending him to slay the dragon Fafnir, but for that he needed a true sword. Sigurd's father had died in battle after being bereft of Gram, which had been broken by Odin, having deemed Sigmund ripe for Valhalla. But the shards were smuggled to safety by the pregnant widow, Hiordis, soon wife of Hialprek, and were reforged by Reginn. For by Sigurd's command, the sword that had slept for a while was to be awoken. With Gram, Sigurd finished off Fafnir to its delight, and in dying Fafnir returned not to dwarvish state. In its first forging Gram had been dullen brown and dragon engraved, prophetic of the brown dragon Fafnir, whose blood it waited long to taste. That sword was destined to become the heirloom of Siward, first cousin to Ulf, the earl of Denmark, and brother-in-law to the great Cnut. Knowing as a true sword when to slay and when to spare, it would teach mercy to Wulfgar, vampire lord. But ah, in the far north Count Drac would have been happy, yet asleep he lay on a bed of clay.

∞

While the Count slept, Wilusa, city of Alaksandu, had been vanquished by Agamemnon. Prince Aeneas and others had escaped, wandering far until welcomed by King Latinus, whose daughter Lavinia he married. In her honour he built the fair city of Lavinium, where Vesta was worshipped. Their son built the long white city of Albalonga. When King Procas died, Numitor, eldest son of Aeneas, should have become king, but his evil brother Amulius defeated him, killed his sons, and forced his daughter to become a priestess of Vesta. Such priestesses were bound by a vow of perpetual celibacy, and thus without slaying her Amulius hoped to end the inheritance line of Numitor who had fled. Yet the true king had the favour of Guardian Malacandra, the earthy wraith of the Cosmic Malacandra, the spirit who oversees the forth planet. Playing the part of husband violated not her vow of celibacy, since her vow foreswore only human husbands, and in high honour she bore twin sons, Romulus—later named after the River Rumon—and Remus, both to the chagrin of her granduncle. Or so the bards have told. Whatever be the truth, in truth great oaks from little acorns grow. Is it any wonder that from small beginnings, the largest empire in the ancient world would rise with legs of iron?

Now by the animus of Amulius these puny twins were to be thrown into the river. But he who was sent to slay foreswore to do that evil, leaving instead the infants down by the riverside, and besought the glorious Guardians to have mercy on the sons of Malacandra and Silvia. At whiles the will of Usen stirs even among the Phusika, and a she-wolf, newly bereft of her cubs, espied the infants as she came to drink, and pity moved her heart—and her self-need also, for she had milk to be drunk. And so she fed them as if her cubs, and played foster-mother unto them. One day, moved by the divinities, Faustulus, swineherd to the king, ventured to her lair, and espying them, took them in joy into his own home, and Larentia his wife raised them as her own. Though knowing who they were, that secret was best kept quiet, even though she would suffer slander from those who thought them hers—for her husband was thrice her age.

Though raised as swineherds—as tough men in a tough land—into noble outlaws they turned, and strayed into the land where Numitor their father lived—yet he knew them not. Remus being captured, was taken before Numitor, who in a dream had been warned to examine his birth. Then Faustulus came to him, kneeling low, and confessed to long knowing of their parentage. Delighted, Numitor sought out Romulus his other son, and in the will of heaven they overthrew Amulius the Usurper, re-enthroning their father. Yet they had dreamed that they must not wait to inherit his domain, but must up and away to seek their own in the land of the she-wolf. Now in that land were seven mountains, east of the Rumon, and here they parted at variance, for divine help seemed unclear. Whether to build on the centre, or on the southern mount, was unclear. And indeed the divine voice speaks either clear or unclear, if it speaks at all—the unclear is to test the wisdom of its hearers. Romulus it was who chose aright. Remus, repenting of his own choice, sought to throw down Romulus, but fierce was his brother that day, and it was Remus who was slain. And the rest, as they say, is history, for *mille vie ducunt hominem per secula Romam!* The Count had missed the road of roads.

∞

Elsewhere there stood a fertile stretch of land, shaped as it were with a head of water, with shoulders and arms of grass, and with chest of sand—like unto a crescent. Into this land the Count had worked evil and brought woe, but now as a Sleepy Joe he missed the show. Within this land many had vied for dominance, and kingdoms had risen and fallen. It knew, and would know, troubling times as if a fierce and furious windstorm from the mouth of Lord Hadad, but the storms were not of Usen's making. The peoples of the land knew shakings as if by the Hammer of Thor, yet it was not of Usen's will. In the ravages that befell the land, many were burned as if by the Fire of Vulcan himself, but Usen was ill-pleased. For those with ears to hear, the raucous laughter of Necuratu could be heard within the woes, but after the fire Usen spoke a brief sound of sheer silence, stirring not the gentle breeze, and in silence he smiled. And his smile warmed the captive land, its shoulders trodden down under the heel of iron. For unto them a child was born, the Sign of Akaz secretly took shape among them.

The Ruach himself had warned the vampires of his intended invasion. To be forewarned is to be forearmed, if you will fight rather than forebear. It was decidedly dangerous to wage open war against their enslaver, Usen the Unjust, but a pre-emptive strike was fully justified. Maybe the Count would have been the chosen one for that attack—who is to say? But though he slept, another was wide awake and on watch, she who among this people had become known as Lilith, she who had ended the life of many an infant, yet protested her innocence. The Ruach was wise, but she thought that the Ruach was too proud for his own good, for he had warned his enemies of their danger, giving them clues that could scupper his plans. One window of opportunity had been given them, location, location, location. He had confirmed it to his miserable students—and he would not lie to them—though the Kingdom of Night studied not their pathetic little lessons. Well, Egypt had risen and fallen and now lay under the iron heel, but since out of Egypt Usen's special son would come, a stakeout there seemed to be the logical imperative, as they watched and waited. An assassination team had been assembled—directly answerable to Lilith—and watched Egypt as Horus himself watched—like a hawk. But there was no sign of their mouse, not even a suspicious bump on the landscape! Lilith herself visited at times, stalking up and down the banks of the Nile, thirsting for that infant's blood, collecting updates: nothing warranted the immediate attention of she who was queen of the Night.

Elsewhere the Ruach, one with Usen the Father and in very essence Usen, had secretly sown a seed that had never before been known, nay nor shall ever again be sown. And so by the operation of the Ruach, the Huion was conceived within time and space, truly one with humanity and in essence truly, yet not only, human. And he was named Hamashiach, the Chosen One, the Game Changer. Born to a vivacious young teenager known only as Miriam, married—and later wedded—to Yosef, whose name protected her son's anonymity, hid his light under a bushel. Yosef's parents scorned her unborn baby as a work of Darkness, and let her in dishonour give birth outdoors. Even they who watched elsewhere for the Light, saw it not. The Ruach's words had been misleadingly true, paradoxical. For Hamashiach indeed came from Egypt, but only because being born elsewhere, he was taken there, then taken away. But the vampires who lived where he was born, weren't on alert; didn't read the signs. When rumours reached Lilith she raced to Egypt, but the bird had flown the coop without trace. Once the local diaboloi cottoned on, they soon picked up the scent, since any new power disturbed their kingdom. Once he became a man with a mission, he was shadowed closely, but aggeloi acted as his personal bodyguard. More oppressively the Ruach lurked close by—unseen but yet still the diaboloi felt him, a dreadful power beyond their power, a stifling scent of death.

Still, at times Hamashiach seemed to be asking for it, and channels of evil incited mob violence against him, or leaguered with his own leaders, though with little success to show for it. Until one day, that is, when they managed to exploit a weakness among his own inner circle. Finally a breakthrough had come, but the kingdoms of Darkness—now talking together for mutual defence—diverged in policy. For the Night counselled that since the prophecy had foretold his execution, then it was imperative that by all means it be prevented: if a prophecy can be broken at any point it is broken. Let him die in fullness of years, a mere professor of ethics. But the Necros argued that Usen was a liar and a cheat. Had he not already spoken deceptively about Hamashiach's birthplace, wrong-footing the opposition? Why assume that that prophecy about him being hoisted on his own handiwork, bespoke crushing as a criminal under the heel of iron? But even if that bit was meant, was it not misinformation to ensure it did not happen, reverse psychology to protect him into fullness of years? No, better by far to take the chance, to exploit the weakness, and rid the earth of him by hook or by crook. Death so far had an enviable record at keeping his prey, and anyway it would be sacrilegious not to seize the chance as a God-send.

"Damned if we don't", the diaboloi said; "damned if you do", the vampires replied! So alone the Necros conspired to terminate him, and rejoiced to see that day. Yet again they were deceived, for unjustly given over to Death he fought back against the injustice, the oppressor, as if death was his chosen theatre of war, and in death defeated death itself—their sole protection. As the prophecy had said, from the chrysalis cave the woodsmith emerged new and indomitable, and arose to deep heaven, untouchable, unstoppable. The dead-end of death no longer offered any kind of protection against Usen, not even for the vampires. A straight-through drive. In his own cave, only a sense of deep disquiet disturbed the heart and mind of the Sleeping Count, who had missed so much.

On Christmas Day of *anno domini* 1,000, Vajk became the new king over Ultra Silvam, where new awakened dwelt a count whom he would never know, a count who arose not by his own power alone. The Count had withered, but then none of the Night were quite what they had been before their bondage to this silent planet. His waking was known by the queen, but was not by the queen. His long sleep had naturally been charmed, that it, entombed by thelodynamic power, an extension of the will of one of Lilith's royal guard, the one tasked with guarding him. Putting him to sleep had been resisted, and other guards had struggled to get him under their trance, but once the Count slept, the power of just one guard had maintained that slumber. True, there had been times when the Count had stirred as a dead man walking. But like stretched elastic, the tenacious tentacles of the tomb had always been able to quickly reassert its will over him, pulling him back from wherever he had wandered, right back into his appointed stupor.

No one but himself really objected to his downtime, but the queen herself was not above criticism. For while happily the Count slept, the hamashiach had come, and gone, defeated and victorious, happy and glorious—on Queen Lilith's watch! Not all her subjects were charitable enough to exonerate her. A tad unfair, because at the end of the day, none of them had foreseen Usen's cunning—he had been too clever by half. They had all been outsmarted and left to smart, so why blame the queen, who in turn blamed the Necros? Unfairly, some did blame her—scapegoats are invaluable.

Among such malcontents were four ladies of the Night no longer, now disinherited. All hoped to regain the Night. All were fair to middling in strength. All became persuaded that if only the Count could be revived, all would be well. Thus it had been that they had conspired together, for it is not unusual that given time, those who mutter aloud will not mutter alone. They thus formed a sisterhood, and these four sisters sought one lord and master, even the great and powerful Count—as they deemed him to be. Over centuries they sought out clues, tried to tap into and trace the thelodynamic waves that bound him in sleep, and in time they succeeded. By that time another malcontent had joined them as a brother. Also of fair to middling power, he had counted on the Count being still as vigorous as he had been in the Nephilim Wars. Together, they had discovered where the undecayed body lay fast bound. Together, they had entered the ancient land of Mordor, to Ultra Silvam, and the secret sealed cavern in which lay Count Drac, undead and dormant. Together, they had wrestled with the power of the royal guard and overcome, freeing the Count. Informed of his escape, the queen had simply decided to let the awoken dog run loose—after all, maybe he had learned his lesson—hope springs eternal in some hearts. His rescuers' hopes had been dashed, however. It had been a bitter disappointment to discover that the catawampus Count was not the Count he had been. He offered little hope of regaining the kingdom, and seemed more interested in gaining human adulation. Indeed, he insisted that his new brides each find a suitable human husband—by suitable, of high rank was meant, but not exceeding his own.

Sensing the queen's tristful tolerance, they remained within—or close to—the land of his imprisonment. It no longer bore the hand of the Dark Lord, and its scars had been weathered clean. Still, it was a land where once the Count had incubated his nascent army, and he happily walked once more along the horseshoe valley's memory lane. The land itself was enough to make the Dark Lord turn in his grave, for what had been his barren and pleasant land had become a pleasant and fertile land to others. However the Dark Lord was no longer in his grave—the Everlasting Dark—but had returned to Arda. He no longer had an outward body to house. He no longer had plans for his ancient lands, nor cared what had become of them, but rather he reflected on how to destroy all lands and yet escape Usen's wrath.

For the Count, the thought of settling in the shadows of that land seemed pleasant enough, integrating into human society, limiting his activities to acceptable levels, cutting according to his cloth, and after some centuries—and Lilith's fall from grace—he cast his gaze upon persons of interest. There was a pleasant breeze of blood in the winds. Violence was king, with sweet promise of more on the way—at least if he played it smart. And so it was that pleased with the rank and disposition of a local count, he stole that count's identity and his life. This of course took many months of preplanning and close shadowing. But then hating to do right, he loved to do wrong right. In this design he worked together with his brother and sisters, each targeting those they wished to replace for their amusement and convenience.

In his new guise as Vlad 2, bastard son of Mircea cel Bătrân of the House of Basarab, he bowed low before his half-brother, Alexandru Aldea, heir of Mircea. Both were of the Church:Orthodox, as befitted their infiltration. They performed religious rites without loving the right. Indeed he who had fathered the real Alexandru and Vlad in Transylvania, had obviously not always been too particular about doing the right, for both these sons were born outside of wedlock, though not perhaps outside of marriage: was it polygamy or was it adultery—who was to say?

Be that as it may, when it came to legitimising the rulership of voivode, viceroy of the king, maternity took back seat to paternity. Nor did the order of birth matter too much. As it was, the younger Alexandru had just been given the job. And under his new identity the Count had just become Vlad the Dragon, Vlad Dracul of the *Societas Draconistarum*, sworn to defend the cross against the crescent. Ironic, he thought, that having begun the days of dragons in Ages past, he should now in human guise pick up a dragon title, extending Drac to Dracul for the present time, and that if he decided to extend his human identity through re-emergence, he'd be a Dracul-a, an heir of Dracul. *C'est la vie*, and his life was much weaker now, so that frequent shape shifts in human form were better avoided. A House of Drăculeşti could live to be feared! His weaker brother was disposable.

In seeming submission he bowed low before his half-brother Alexandru, but telepathically spoke silent words of warning: "Come brother, I am content that you rule in name, but I, who am your better, command that you take this land into war with the Turks. Why should you hold off? Why seek the peace of the land, when we revel in bloodshed?"

"No, Count. You were enslaved to sleep for causing too many calamities among the human kind. You who are but recently emancipated, do you dare to create havoc under the watchful eye of the queen? She knows where we are and what we do. I fear that her permissive will will not allow overindulgence. These are early days. Already you have enjoyed the blood of these people. Be content. Let us do nothing that rulers should not do, lest her wrath be stirred. If you fall this time, we might all fall into the short sleep of death—and then? Besides, Alexandru, whom I replaced, would have sought peace at the price of paying off the sultan, as befits one born of mild Miss Maria. We committed to act in character, did we not?"

"Yes, but not to the point of not having a little fun! Let war wet our fangs once more."

"Do you think me a killjoy, Count? I am not, but the time is not ripe to break out in bloody slaughter. We must satisfy the queen that our bloodlust is under control. The Dragon Order is bound by oath to fight the Muslim dominators, but only if to defend the church if attacked, and if the chance of success is reasonable enough to justify war. Who with 10,000 should attack an army of 20,000, if all else is equal? No, our army is outnumbered, and we must not endanger our own lives among these primitive people, for our shapes are mortal, and the people are many."

Neither brother departed in a happy frame of mind. On the one hand, the Count deemed his brother unworthy of the name brother, and pondered how to be rid of him—discreetly, lest he worried his brides or jeopardised his own human persona. On the other hand, Alexandru was annoyed with his bothersome brother; no longer glad with Vlad. Rangda, who had recently taken the throne from Lilith, was unlikely to stir into action unless the banished were overly troublesome to the human world, undermining the secrecy of the Night. He did not wish to be put to sleep for another's sin, and sincerely hoped that Vlad had seen sense.

But Alexandru was just too naive for his own good, vainly hoping that Vlad's quiescence boded well. Vlad played it smart. He went quiet, outwardly playing second fiddle in the human realm to his brother, the voivode of Wallachia, to the south of Transylvania. And Alexandru played it smart with the Ottomans, submitting as a vassal. His human resources were insufficient to break free, and if he fought outgunned he himself might die, which would displease him immensely. He had little leeway to use his vampire powers, either to build up his army or to undermine the Ottomans'. So he must play it cool, play the waiting game. Meanwhile, there was plenty of free range food, easy pickings, even if no real fun on the side. Rivers of blood would just have to wait.

But Vlad it seemed, could not wait. Within five years Count Dracul flew one dark night into Alexandru's castle unobserved, hung around until the noon sun when Alexandru was quietly resting, and unseen by mortal man made good the murder of his brother. The physician on call was obviously too late to consult the *Vademecum*, as there was the corpse, stone cold, lying in its bed, and neither apothecary nor leech would bring back the voivode now. Alexandru had had a hearty breakfast, though as usual had then retired to his room, locking it from the inside so as to be alone and undisturbed, as was his wont. It was only late afternoon that the door had been forced, for he had ignored both the early notice bells announcing the evening meal, and his guard hammering on the door. Examination of the body showed no signs of physical injury, so the only reasonable verdict was death following some imbalance between the external elements of earth, fire, water, and air, with their corresponding bodily humours of black bile, yellow bile, phlegm, and blood which carried all four elements, perhaps caused by a hex—but the physician would not positively swear to it.

Vlad 2 at last asserted his right to be the voivode of Wallachia, and was duly installed. Now at last he could raise an army to fight the Turk. He had no special down on Turks, and had he been awakened among them, would have as happily fought the cross as the crescent. Who he fought was not as important to him as the mere fact of fighting, especially when the alternative was to live in subjection, or at least subjection to a assumed enemy, as Turkey-land was so clearly to his people. He would not be scorned as a coward, he who loved to see blood run red. But first he stole to the tomb of Alexandru, for by his will his brother was in stasis, still holding onto his body although unable to reanimate it, his very telepathy gagged. The Count then removed the head, releasing the spirit from its body: and thus Alexandru the Vampire really did die and depart unto the final judgment. Such base treachery would be scorned by his own kind, even by his brides if they discovered the dastardly trick. It was also a foolish, some might say childish, slaying, for although Alexandru was the weaker, he might still have proved a useful ally.

As it was, Vlad Dracul aimed to get tough with Sultan Murad, but due to unforeseen circumstances found himself having to kowtow to him instead, even joining in the Muslim invasion of Transylvania. Very humiliating! Only then did he realise that perhaps Alexandru had understood *realpolitik*—ah well, too late to bring back the departed. But he felt repressed. It didn't satisfy his ego to simply graze content upon his own subjects, so when invited by the voivode of Transylvania to drive out the Muslim invader, he was all too eager to say yes. Unfortunately that fight against the Turk hadn't gone too well, and facing an angry sultan he had agreed to leave two sons under Muslim control, hostages in token of future compliance. Yet it hadn't been a complete defeat, since his sons would act as his eyes and ears within the Ottoman Empire. But next time Transylvania asked his help, he turned a blind eye of indifference. He did however, soon cross the Danube in favour of the crusading bull following Buda's diet, fighting in a European union against Muslim expansionism, a war that he believed stood a better chance of success: he hated defeat.

Yet that war did not end in expelling the Muslim forces, and the Dragon actually made his peace yet again with the sultan, this time much to the disgust of Transylvania's John Hunyadi, who became his mortal enemy. And Hunyadi it was who seemingly slew the Dragon— yet it was not so. Under that cover of death, Count Dracul worked next through the two of his sons whom he had enslaved to his will, in particular one whose nature most corresponded to his own, one who had learned the Muslim skill of impalation. That son would soon make that signature skill his special trademark, for he was ever too keen to employ what should never have been more than a punishment of last resort. Weep for Vlad the Impaler, sadistic slave-son, through whom the Dragon arose as Vlad Dracul-a, Dragon-son.

But happy was the dragon to have such a son, and happily they worked side by side to make the name Dracula a name of terror and of loathing to the Muslim hordes. When his demented son was finally put out of his misery, his head was felled from his body and served up to the sultan on a silver plate. Though his slavery to his father had ended, his slavery to himself alone had just begun. Still, the Count did not cry over such loss. He had seen blood soaked fields, and his enemy weep, and that had felt good. In times to come he would recount this gory story of glory, as if his very own story—but then in spirit it was. The *drăculeşti*, adopting his sobriquet, lived on, and his body remained hidden among them.

His brides had their own stories to tell. As vampires, they too were creatures aged in billennia, not decades, and much evil they had enjoyed, even before the dawn of man. How did they fare under the Count? As said, each at some point married counts, adopting the ways of humanity, complying with the Count's command to interact with the trash. Partly he reasoned that Queen Rangda would not wish to muddy her hands in human affairs, but in some ways he seemed to his brides to be rather childish, even puerile. But he was now their lord and master, and they had all gotten considerably weaker, needing to hang together for mutual comfort and support. Resting alongside humans had its advantages. It was to be that none truly loved their husbands—it would have shamed them otherwise. But a dark husband could share the vampire taste for fun. Such had been the husband of Erzsébet Báthory, Countess of Fogarasfold. As was the vampire way, the real Erzsébet had been transplanted, and her identity assumed.

Happily Erzsébet had been bullied by girls in her youth, and the imposter's human husband had a taste for blood, both facts allowing her the liberty to act as one seeking a blood revenge on the world. Happily she had feasted on sadistic fetishes, unhindered and encouraged by her husband, Ferenc. Girls and women, especially among the peasant class, could be quite easily toyed with and disposed of, and Erzsébet became adept at torturing them for her amusement. Besides, Ferenc had put his foot down, forbidding her to torture boys or men—perhaps he had feared that if acclimatised to do so, he might one day fall as her prey.

Rangda would not intervene, the more so as Erzsébet had merged into a human setting, seemingly a sadistic countess in a sadistic world. Nor was the world likely to intervene, since she had joined the political elite and could literally get away with murder. And that is in fact just what she did. Not quick, painless murder, but long, excruciatingly long, dying. She who treated her victims as subhuman was *unmenschlich*. The depth of her depravities need not, nay, should not, be recounted here. Suffice to say that she wallowed in blood and gore—by the tub load. Some said that she even bathed in blood—for her beauty—and she was beauteous to the naked eye. But if the eye could see into her heart, what rotting hideousness would have been revealed. Woe to them who fell into her clutches, whose fate she sealed. She was unrepentant, indeed triumphant, she who dressed in the coat of the Dragons.

Yet she overreached herself, moving from peasantry to lesser nobility, and tried by nobility was condemned to be sealed in until death. Yet such was her power that the sealing remained little more than confinement within her own castle of Csejte, until she allowed her body to die in 1614 anno domini. It was removed, by public insistence, far away, being interred in the Báthory family crypt, where it was intended that it should see corruption. Yet soon she had bodily left that crypt and re-joined the Count, revelling in her stories. Unlike Ferenc, under the Count men were once more on the menu, but though men could be toyed with more pleasingly than youngsters, more often it was children or infants, less likely to be missed by many.

They all had their favourite New Age stories, of course. One, often recalled during family fun time, was that of Agnes, Countess of Helfenstein. "She was a fool!" she chuckled to the Count.

"Ah," said he, "you mean the late lamented Lenore, I think. Yes she was, but it felt good to bury her." She always began the telling of that story the same way.

"It was but chance that I passed by her hovel when *ihre mutter* was berating her" continued Agnes. "If her mother predicted her damnation, who was I to gainsay it?" The Count chuckled. The story had often been retold, but still held its pristine pleasure. It had followed in the wake of yet another war waged—among humans the follies of the few easily led to the slaughter of the many, if the few had power over the many. The witlessness of man was ever strange to vampires, who valued their mortal lives much more—perhaps because they feared the judgment beyond death much more. Plenty of fun to be had lingering around the battle fields, especially among the unattended dying.

But also the dark vampires could capitalise on families left without sons, husbands, and fathers. In 1763 a young damsel named Lenore had grieved that her intended had not returned from the war. Taught that Usen was an interventionalist, as a simpleton she slagged him off, for, she said, if he directs every arrow and bullet in battle, he must have targeted William the tailor, her betrothed. At the opposite end of the spectrum, the deists would have completely exonerated him, by insisting that he had absolutely nothing further to do with his creation—non-interventionalism. She would not have understood that lot, for she was no scholar.

"That you curse he who is The Eternal damns you in this life and the next", mimicked the Count, quoting what Lenore's horrified mother had said, as if Usen were some sort of petty egotist. There hadn't been much debate, for neither mother nor daughter really knew how to. Instead, both sides merely repeated their respective positions until they were both blue in the face. Probably nothing more would have come from their futile chitter chatter, had Agnes not overheard it in passing. Such stupidity invited a bit of fun, and she enjoyed recounting the story. They all knew it by heart. The Count's point was blatantly obvious.

"Yes, that that that that that mother said was sooo silly, pales in comparison to the stupid girl's gullibility in swallowing it hook, line, and sinker, simply showing how silly Usen is to put up with such dopey creatures", Agnes chuckled. "But I must go on. It was all such a jolly feast of fun, especially after I called you in. For you reshaped yourself as rider, and I as horse, and swiftly we bore the dumb damsel—as if you were her William riding to her bridal chamber—swiftly to her burial chamber—*die todten reiten schnell*. There I opened up a grave especially for her, and we buried her in the sure and certain knowledge of her dying despair."

That at least was how they preferred to remember it. The fact that poor Lenore had, in dying breath, begged Usen for mercy, soured the joke somewhat, but that she died smothered in the ground as a simpleton, still tickled their humour. As to Usen's plan for his children after their deaths, even vampires didn't really know, but the going idea was that somehow he would feed on them, that death somehow enriched their *élan vital* to make them palatable. Who can read the mind of Usen?

Vampires of the Night feasted on fatuity, even more than on fear, delighted in the idea that Usen's foolery was evident in bothering about such stupid, ephemeral creatures, while enslaving smart Simbolinians. "And what story have you to tell us, Countess Lacrimal?"

"That I, lover of men—as ever widow spider loves her mates on which she dines—did even perfect a way into young women's hearts. As Millarca I married and 'died'. A century or so later, as a mere chit of a girl, I stalked for play a young girl named Laura, a descendent of mine, bewildering and beguiling her emotions. For I played the part of a man with a maid—yet as a maid calling black white and white black—and still she could not quite escape my lure, ensnared in a girlish crush for my mystique. Quoth she: 'Girls are but caterpillars in the world, but fly as butterflies when their summer comes. Until then they are but grubs and larvae, don't you see—each with their peculiar propensities, necessities, and structure.' It was not her humility that amused me, but the fact that she actually believed that butterflies are anything more than bugs with wings.

"As Carmilla, I stayed at Laura's house, spellbinding her insensible sire, sleeping in the day and dining at nights: my locked doors baffled them, but what are locks to we whose wills can turn locks without keys? On the whole a delightful holiday, dumbfounding a daughter who claimed discernment, and draining dull damsels. Yet their funerals were intolerable, strangulating the sensitive by songs diabolical. Even some of them hate their uncouth hymns, though their singing's gone global! Sadly my stay was cut short. A man whose daughter I had sucked dry spoilt my fun, preventing the *coup de grace*, having the nerve to even seek my head! The real Countess Karnstein's body lay buried against such a move, preserved undead amidst two hand-spans of stay-fresh blood. While they vented their fury—and compassion—on what was neither their enemy nor needing their friendship, I stood quietly hidden in the shadows, enjoying the farce of impaling the body's heart, removing its head, then burning the whole job lot! I even threw my scream at that superstitious lot, for I would not have liked that done to me."

"Yet," the Count chuckled, "if they kill us by their superstition, we can still die laughing. Their crassness remains a choice source of conviviality among us. For instance, somehow it leaked out that I am allergic to garlic, *ipso facto* all vampires must be, say those who have some smattering of our story and seek our deaths. I say this, yet I utterly deny that they have discovered us through me. It is plain that some of the Dawn Kingdom have revealed our identity—the more reason to kill the traitors. Curse them! Come, Countess of Gratz, tell us a merry tale before we dine."

But the shade of Countess Dolingen was nowhere to be found. She had been rather withdrawn for some time, perhaps in a bit of a miff, and the Count, truth be told, had grown tired of her carping ways. She had intervened between him and some victims a short while ago, and he had merely punished her by imprisoning her body in a marble tomb, staking it out like one might pin a moth. Admittedly a wee bit harsh, but his wives needed to be kept under his control, and should know that it was for their own good. Boy, a nagging wife was like water going drip-drip-drip on a rainy day! He'd have a few more words to say to her another day, but now was not the time to fly off the handle.

"Well, shall I tell you a tale concerning her? Once upon a time, shortly before I became Dracula but after I had become Dracul, I was accosted by two seemingly innocent travellers. They had come from an island in the west, and had traded some years within sight of my castle walls. Then in guise as merchants they begged audience, claiming to have recognised a spy of the sultan's among us. Of course their eyes betrayed their kind, and I sensed their greater power, especially the woman's. Had they been assassins, I would not be here now, but they claimed to be Hamashiachim. My hatred of the Dawn Kingdom is as love compared to my contempt for that revolting kind, for it is most unreasonable and anaemic. To put ones hands into a wolf's maw is to live without hands. To not even threaten the wolf with fire, or drought, or to turn water into blood, or to curse with some plague! Bah, weakness and ineptitude. All they threatened was to bore me to death with pleadings, as if my soul was at stake.

"Thus Faramundo and Ishtar stood before me, as helpless as two bunnies before a wolf. For were not you, my brides, ready at my beck and call? Together we might outmatch them, or so I judged. But am I not as wise as a wolf? News they gave me of the turncoat Lókestámo, rebranded as Alessandro, who had last been heard of helping a forest robber within some petty realm of man. It was sweetly satisfying news to hear! So, Alessandro has gallingly suffered great humiliation, reduced to serving man instead of enslaving man. How the mighty had fallen! An unhappy enemy pleases the soul, but they claimed the absurdity that in servitude he was fulfilled, and invited me to bow the knee! They claimed to invite me into the Day, but I saw through their subterfuge. They who had come from a deposed queen, did they not seek my alliance to regain her throne?

"Feigning sincerity, of Hamashiach they pleaded passionately, as if their hero. A hero, who had invited his own death? Death did not tempt me! I let them blether on. How could they really believe that Usen's messenger should be trusted any more than Usen, he who had imposed on us the Eighth Law? To that they could give no clear answer. They ventured that the Law might bind us to this world as a plaster to a wound, to accomplish some unknown healing in some unknown future. But how does the wound help the plaster, I asked? They replied that though the wound needs its help, that afterwards both the healed and the healer might rejoice together. But why should we, who lived when the Children were as slime, wish to share the happiness of weaklings? They had become the wounded, not we. They replied that Usen had imposed weakness upon the Children that they should mature through suffering. It was to me as if these two were wounded in their heads, revelling in and recommending weakness.

"By guile I separated them for a space—divide and conquer. It was then that together we overcame them, first the one, then the other. And what joy we had, for such drivellers had been diseased, their bodies fit only to litter the streets. But more hurt we took than should have been—for well they fought to flee. For Dolingen had half-heeded their miserable message. She begged me to spare them, for she said she had been terribly disturbed by a dream about them—had she read my mind? She even threatened to take their part, to fight alongside them against us. Traitor!

"Four against three would have made bad odds, when five against one was what I counted on. My wits did not desert me. For thus by my will we took poor Dolingen to a ghost town I owned near Monachium, for there I had had prepared a tomb for her body's first sleep, hoping a second entombment would never be needed to sort out her mind. Thus we four then fought Faramundo first, having wiled Ishtar away on a fool's mission. His thelodynamic power taxed us, but at last we had the upper hand. But when Ishtar returned and sought for him, then we were sorely tried. How had such a mighty fallen into error or deceit?

"Yet praise be to the Dark, we were triumphant without Dolingen to aid or to thwart. Perhaps her shade has slunk away lest she had been called on to recount the story of her first infamy, or her second which returned her body to her tomb. Long I think it shall be, until she can be trusted again to work hand in glove with us, but you my brides I honour. And now, the sun sets on the world outside. It is time to wander—though remember to remain in sight of this castle."

Lilith had commanded, and Rangda had confirmed, that the Count be confined to barracks, at least to feed: unwisely he had gluttonised when he should merely have grazed, gorging on human blood. The Night was canny about the Children being overly aware of its existence. Because the imprudent Count had rocked the boat, not the cradle, the Night had penalised him for overtaxing the human herd of Wallachia. The herd was harried, and the tongues of surviving witnesses wagged.

By royal command, the Count alone had been threatened with high treason unless he changed his ways, moderated his approach to life, and gave the sheep more slack. In short, he was allowed to survive, but only by guile—only those who willingly entered his house, whether humble or high, would be his lawful prey. That is not to say that he didn't bend the rules a little, sneakily snacking on the side. But by and large he complied. When Rangda became queen, she treated him just as badly, perhaps fearing him too much to let him fly free. If so, she didn't realise how powerless he had become: he was no longer up to running the leadership race. Anyway, being suppressed, he had insisted that his brides likewise be largely confined to their homebase. There was plenty of fodder in the surrounding mountain villages, although they had to be rationed. For treats he sometimes allowed them to tantalise and to torment guests within his castle.

Their lockdown might last ten to twenty thousand years, but as long as they stayed at home, stayed safe, they could hope for time off for good behaviour. Storytelling helped them to pass the daytimes and to relive the past, but they were still allowed nighttimes to stretch their wings. So the girls went out to play under the pale moon. Seldom nowadays did they eat out, since the Count was a stern husband to them, even as Rangda was a stern queen to him. He had lost all except his life, and he did not mean to lose that. And at last he had an escape plan. Probably the queen spied on him, but probably sporadically. So couldn't he slip by the radar, shake off the shadow? His memory not being as it used to be, he had taken to writing down events in a secret diary. Dates were sparingly used, since a *terminus a quo* reminded them of a *terminus ad quem*. Besides, 'what' seemed more important than 'when'. The Count and countesses combined human centuries with their own system of chronicling, but *anno domini* rubbed new salt in old wounds.

C19T ΞΔ: Count Dracula[i]   154

Yesterday Dolingen sneaked off, we know not where. After story-time I summoned her violently, but she replied not. Had she obediently not gone far but refused to answer, or disobediently gone far but not refused to answer? Is it not enough that I have staked out her body, forbidding her from freeing it? These fools hold to me for their safety, yet itch to stray as if safe. Their skills exceed the human lot, but their power is little more, though brides I call them. Fools—but I need them as a buffer zone. Dolingen I might yet flog, if ever I allow her her body back. Whereas there is no shame is expelling a wife, there is shame in losing one, but in front of the others I pretend to be unperturbed.

C19T ΞE: Count Dracula   155

Several days have passed since Dolingen disappeared. Deciding to investigate whether she might have attempted to regain her body, I flew to Monachium. There her body lies as one dead, staked out with my seal. Indeed it should cry out to me if it breaks, and while unbroken will enforce my will on the body. Her second entombment is well deserved, and she is rightly chastised. Yet if she comes to heel I will still welcome her back. Her sisters would happily slay her, for they know that she still ponders the life of the Light. But if not to regain her body, where might she be? Hiding from me? I planned her no ill. Scheming for her part? But without her body she is so limited, almost impotent. Has she simply succumbed to rightful shame, so that she can no longer face us? That would be satisfying.

C19TΞZ: Count Dracula   156

Questioning the Lady Lacrimal, I discovered that Dolingen, my Countess of Gratz, dared to darken my private domain on the very night before she departed. If she has read from my journal stone, the situation could be serious. Plans are afoot to wrong foot Rangda's agents and to escape. An agent from Exeter in England, seeks to visit me soon—a telegram today gives details. If Dolingen has read of my plans, does she intend to frustrate them? They centre around a certain Mr Harker, whom I have yet to have the pleasure to meet. Though a weak link, that weakness meets my need for secrecy well. But if that old bat should get to him first, derail him by warning or by wound, this chance will be lost, and making another risks rousing Rangda. I have placed the countesses at roughly equidistant spaces between here and Monachium, though telepathic communication will be unavoidably patchy. There, Agnes, my Countess of Helfenstein, can watch over Mr Harker, and ensure his safe arrival. At Bécs, Lacrimal, my Countess of Karnstein, might even pick up her presence—if she has returned to Gratz. At Ecséd, Erzsébet, my Countess of Fogarasfold, is well placed to forward messages to and from me. Perdition be praised, my Journal had made no reference to where Mr Harker is to come from, merely that he is to arrive first at Monachium. That the termagant has gone to trap him there cannot be doubted—Necuratu necrotize her!

C19TO: Count Dracula   160

I notice that my jottings have become more daily than yearly, reflecting my hopes and fears moving apace. I had not counted on Erzsébet seeking to reassert herself in Ecséd, instead of seeking my will. I will spit and roast her if she fails me again, for she gave me days of sleeplessness, wondering whether either countess upline had spotted the errant Dolingen. This night came news. Mr Harker had arrived early from Caletum, coincidentally on the day before Agnes usually takes her annual Monachium holiday. Fortunately for her, she promises to refrain from festivity until the victim is within my grasp.

She went not to fight Dolingen—the stronger of the two when bodied. As my messenger she did her job, reporting back.

C19ΠZ: Countess Dolingen   76

Not in vain have I watched and waited, for I have sighted the target, and hope to kill two birds with the one stone, as some say. Clearly Count Dracula seeks to escape the queen's eye, exposing his brides to punishment, with him or without him. Whether or not he simply means to abandon us to our fates, I have jumped before being pushed. Yet ever since two of our people sought him out, claiming to seek only his wellbeing, have I not been pushed? They contradicted the Night, for to us the wellbeing of another matters only if it is for mutual wellbeing. We did not trust them, therefore, but why did they claim such nonsense, endangering their own lives? I counselled him to chase them away: even if Usen sought to deceive, why risk his revenge by eliminating his messengers? In fury he entombed my body, and has done so yet again: I suspect that he has similar in store for my sisters, should they in turn lose his favour. Apoplectically he said that I have sought death, and that by all that is unholy, by my sin against the Night, I have found it! Yet maybe he is less ready to punish my sisters, for though he is weakened little by the removal of one, he would be weakened much by the removal of four. My body and I have been separated now for some time, and though in desperation I would now disobey him and reunite body and soul, he has set up thelodynamic barriers that without my bodily access I cannot break, and with my bodily access would have no need to break. I have a plan. Since I must kill his target, I might as well use him first—the tomb is not man-proof.

C19ΠΘ: Countess Dolingen   78

I watched over the man Harker all night, reading and writing his mind. Like us he is one who delights not in travel but in new sights, but these people are limited to land and sea, save some few who have ventured above land or below water. Will they ever rise above their own world, seeing it as we have seen it? For my purpose he must first venture out this day to a nearby village. My will has still some power over weather, which perhaps will help manoeuvre Harker to unlock the first door. If this plan fails me, I fear that I shall fail and fall: he will not spare me for arranging my escape by disarranging his.

C19TOA: Count Dracula   161

The Countess Dolingen be damned! Wilfully that witch almost wrecked my plans. Revenge must wait. I must abide in my castle. I must not draw unwanted attention. Agnes has proved that she is worth her weight in gold, or at least in silver. Though allowing the shade of Dolingen to mesmerise Mr Harker, she prevented any real harm. Dolingen had lured him out for a pleasure ride, but when informed I read the danger, and neutralised it. For Dolingen had led Mr Harker as a bull by the nose to be slaughtered, straight to Agnes' holiday village—purged of its superstitious people some little while ago—and to her own tomb. It was only by the mysterious change in weather that my slave realised the danger, and in wolf's shape hastily visited the tomb.

There she found that Mr Harker had been coaxed by the elements unto the mouth of the tomb. The shade of Dolingen withstood her, so at first she did but howl her protest from afar. My barriers against Dolingen's shade fell like dominoes, once Mr Harker had pressed open the bronze door. I had not counted on any human daring to approach the village, let alone forcing the tomb. Breaking the door's seal weakened my binding power, allowing her to fly as a shattering lightning bolt straight through the iron staked roof, snapping my will that kept her body and soul apart. Re-embodied, she would surely have drained the unfortunate young man dry, had not my agent regained her nerve and, still as a wolf, opposed the will of Dolingen, fighting not for Mr Harker's soul but for his body: they are mine.

C19ΠΙ: Countess Dolingen79

This night I rest all too near to Monachium, fearing for my life. My plans have met with success and failure. Success, in that almost beyond hope I have regained my body. Failure, in that Harker yet lives, and if the Count has his way with him, then I fear that the queen's hand will be heavy on all who have sided with the Count. Perhaps my treason towards the Count will be counted as loyalty to the Crown, which in truth was loyalty only to me. I am in double jeopardy from Crown and Count. To hide is simply to put off the evil day of reckoning, but has that not always been the way of vampires?

Curse the Count, I had almost succeeded. His binding spell was broken, the static enveloping of his power snapped. Instantly my physical and astral bodies reunited, but sadly sister Agnes dragged Harker away from me before I could caress him in my arms and drain him dry to the last bone—only one delightful taste did I manage. Then the wretched she-wolf opposed me. I read her mind—the cowardly Count had sent a woman to do a man's job, while he lay sniffling in his castle for fear of the queen. Agnes alone I knew I could tackle and must, though the reintegration, the replanting, wilted me somewhat. Yet access to my old power was reawakening, the focus of my thelodynamic power was coming into calibration. But no time did the Count allow, for troopers appeared through the bushes, summoned by him and directed by her. We both fled in different directions, leaving the Count's guest free.

∞

Between the machinations of the two vampires, Mr Jonathan Harker had been brought into play, as might yet spell loss to the Dark Side. The following day he took the train to Bécs, where the countesses of Helfenstein and Karnstein would together shadow him safely to the Count in Transylvania. Not knowing where Dolingen might lurk, they closely shadowed him as he explored the city, gazing in unalloyed admiration at its bridges, and the noble width and depth of the Danube they spanned. Nor did they leave door or window unguarded at the majestic Hotel Royale, their minds scanning adjoining rooms, floors, and ceilings, against three dimensional attack—Lacrimal paced as a sleepless dog below his window. He travelled with his unseen guards to the town of Bistritz, and from there by coach through the Borgo Pass.

C19P: Countess Dolingen 80

As with my former entry, I see no way to get at the victim. Indeed it is now close guarded by my three blind sisters. Do they not see that the Count will lie lower if he lies in secret, so will look to escape from them as well as from Rangda? And because of him, and without him, will they survive the queen's anger? But they are blind indeed, satisfied by him for the morsels he throws their way. The chance of getting to Harker before the Count, looks increasingly improbable. I continue to shadow them, for improbable is not impossible.

C19TOΓ: Count Dracula   163

One was good; two were better; three are best. I can almost smell his blood. There cannot now be any doubt but that my slaves will soon deliver Mr Harker to me safe and sound. But indeed, as he must be neither freed nor felled, neither must he be forced, since it may be that the queen's agents watch over all comers to my humble halls. "Will you walk into my parlour?" has been my long refrain. Those who venture my winding stair, never come down again. I'll put them all to long last sleep, drink blood until they wane. All who rest on feather bed, my comely wives shall drain.

If he refuses to enter, I dare not pursue him, but I can inspire him with such fear without, that he strongly seeks his safety within. Besides, he has a commission to seek me out, and came without any doubts. The local peasants fear me, but fear the unknown world more. Hopefully they will keep their fears to themselves, but Englishmen put little weight on the fanciful fears of foreigners—that would be so un-British! The fool! But a gentleman I shall be, even a gentleman's gentleman.

∞

From the Golden Krone Hotel, Jonathan Harker began his penultimate carriage journey. He was forewarned and forearmed by superstition: in local belief the Count was either a diabolos or a diabolist. But what is a crucifix to a vampire, any more than to a mosquito? Both be bloodsuckers; both can be deadly. Yet a mosquito hates not a crucifix—though can be slain by it—while those of the Night hate the crucifix—though cannot be slain by it. Yet they who are not repulsed by battle, are repulsed by the sign of their defeat. If the weaker lose cohesiveness by the fear of it, they are undone not by the power of the icon, but by the power of their fear. The Count—unlike his wives—was more at risk from anaphylactic reaction to garlic! Jonathan was armed by symbol and scent, the weak and the strong. But once summoned, unto the dragon's den he rode; into the valley to death was he driven.

Yet the road to death was paved with beauty: blossom of apple, plum, pear, and cherry; the green grass, the majestic mountains. Hand in hand with sickness and sacredness, as ever those two walk together, looking down and up through mortal life. But the unease of oppression began weighing down the clouds, as if they rode towards the very thunder of Thor. The sun had yielded her power to the night, and the only stars were those of man, bedecking their carriage, illuminating the lathered horses that stove to eat up the miles—obeying the urgent message of the whip. At the transfer point, no sign was seen of the Count's carriage. Jonathan was urged to not wait, but to abide as a passenger until his carriage reached its terminal. He vaguely suspected that his driver had arrived early in order to depart early in order to avoid the Count, when out of the darkness the Count's calèche swept suddenly into view. There seemed no escape for the lonely lamb.

C19TO∆: Count Dracula 164

The fiends sought to whisk him from under my nose without even a taster. Uncivil louts! Within my domain the very wolves hear my voice and speak my words. My sentinels espied their haste from afar, giving me just scant time to rendezvous at the pickup point before they departed. But at last he was all but mine, for what alternative had he—to take his chance with the wolves and the weather? As dismal driver, I elatedly drove him home, zigzagging to determine whether Dolingen tracked us. The countesses were wearied and had retired directly to the castle to prepare welcome. My wolves sensed my elation, and sang with me. It stirred my soul to hear their song, though it agitated my horses, which I had not bothered to bend to my will. The feebleness of the human race vexes me, but a lamb who wilts before my sheep dogs' song will not dare leave his butcher's side—pitiful humans.

He shall serve as both *le plat principal*, and *le digestif*, my business before my brides' pleasure. My bride-wolves thus sang their welcome as we neared my castle, but they could become an enemy within. Without were the blue lights of the firstborn, warning me that I am watched: will they never forgive the Nephilim War? Mr Harker was curious, but since he entered of his own free will, a cock-and-bull story I can tell. Though the night is young, I am not, and shall sleep well when the daylight comes, the happier knowing that the rabbit is in the cage.

C19PB: Countess Dolingen   82

I fear that the victim is all but dead to me. I care less than a jot for him, even as I care not a toss for a tool but only for what it does. Would that I had managed to break it before it reached Dracula's hand. I expended vital energy in the enterprise of regaining my somatic body, but my strength returns rapidly, and embodied I will soon be as strong as ever—and I might soon need to be. Never has fly escaped such a spider, but there seems to be something special about this fly. If against hope he escapes, there are besiegers who might ward off the hunting spider. They love not the brides of the Count, but maybe they will suffer me to collaborate in order to circumvent the Count's designs. I must face their fury; they must see me as an enemy of their enemy.

C19TOE: Count Dracula   165

My guest is safe within my web. In my welcome he saw my pleasure, but does not understand. He suffers the blindness of a solicitor—inside their limited brief they see brightly enough, but outside can be clueless. Up into my parlour we went, but his time to dine has not ended. He will guess that I escorted him here, but my doors open easier inwards than outwards. I am deeper in his debt than he realises or desires, and he deserves—and shall have—my most courteous attention. I shall put his mind at ease. He seemed to study my appearance as a rabbit fixedly studies the fox: this is my lair, not his burrow—he cannot escape.

C19TOZ: Count Dracula   166

Mr Harker has enquired about our lack of servants and mirrors. I replied that as to servants, they are but few, and by chance some enjoy vacation, some attend family needs. That as to mirrors, they are but a vomitous vanity. I play the eccentric, the somewhat miserly yet gracious host. Arising early from my slumber I found him in my English library. One of his functions is to teach me a fluency in the spoken language, to better fit into London's genteel society, casting off my Transylvanian tongue, its ways for their ways. He has an inquisitive mind, but I can fob him off when needs be. He must neither flee, nor panic—yet. All bodes well for my transfer to an out-of-the-way estate of the small town of Purfleet, east of the capital city. I made a flying visit some months ago, and instructed my Exeter agent in ways that led him to discover it for himself. There I met a squatter, a Mr Renfield, educated, but escaped from creditors. He has become a temporary slave, for he might be of some use. By contrast Mr Harker is young and gay, and speaks of his delights as if I must share them—human arrogance from which I will shortly deliver him. Shades and shadows shall be his lot, in place of sunshine and sparkling waters. We spoke until the sun rose.

C19TOH: Count Dracula   167

Using a shaving mirror he had brought—I need them not—Mr Harker was visibly startled by what must have been my lack of visibility in the mirror. My body is in the visible world, so naturally reflects, but in the invisible world I doubt not that spiritual nothingness awaits me. That Usen—for the diaboloi give this gift only to their tools—gave him brief clairvoyance, disturbed me. Is his girlfriend praying for him, invoking the Enemy? Instinctively I clutched at him as if to end this danger, but seeing his little crucifix, immediately released him, realising with relief that he was still safely under superstation's spell. But he is not so safe. Why, while shaving he clumsily laid bare his blood, and like sharks, my beautiful brides are not to be overly trusted. He must shave no more.

C19TOI: Count Dracula   169

I still remain amused at my rat, though time has flown by. I continue to wait upon him hand and foot, deeds which in human thinking would be beneath my rank, but we use human rank merely as tools, and the rank of pauper can be as useful as the rank of prince. In return I have gleaned useful knowledge, not least about Whitby, upon which I have some design, and to which I have written to a Mr Billington. Mr Harker nicely clutches onto superstition, and it firmly grips him. He sometimes fingers his peasant's crucifix, as if to ward off evil: I feel so much safer when he snuggles up within its false sense of security.

C19TΠ: Count Dracula   170

Perhaps I erred in letting him keep his trinket, for by his unexpected venturesomeness he imperilled his meaningless life and my meaningful plans. I had forbidden part of my castle to him, and part to my brides, that ne'er the twain should meet. Doubtless trusting in his crucifix, he dared to darken their domain. In their own luminance they allured him, as they love to bedazzle all the buffoons I send them. My blonde bombshell Agnes tried to claim the right of first use of the helpless buck, his defences cast down by his own captivation to their charms. Rescued in the nick of time, he stirred and stuttered to me that her eyes were of the same pale blue sapphire as the wolf that rescued him. Cannot he put two and two together and make four? For my part I almost turned the vixen's eyes black in my fury. Well they know that he is not yet for them—can they not wait, that pack of wolves? They spoke of love—not the human feelings which are anathema to them and to me, but of play with the human body! Faugh! Did I not have child by sindeldi maid in the spawning of the nephilim? They but mocked the scars I gained when that venture came to naught. I merely insist that they play not with Mr Harker until I have played my game through Mr Harker. They mustn't know my plans. He has had a close shave. Their mesmeric affect has dazed his senses, but he will soon regain full sight.

C19TПГ: Count Dracula 173

Mr Harker now lives nicely in the fear that his elimination is nigh. Since he attempted to smuggle out a coded letter to Miss Wilhelmina through my Romanis—doubtless a cry for rescue—I took steps to prevent him from smuggling himself out. Now I have taken steps to smuggle myself out. My brides have again invited him to play, but my bunny preferred its burrow to my she-wolves. Showing less sense, the mother of a child I fed them shared its fate, though her flesh fed real wolves. Admirably she showed more spunk than has my rabbit.

C19TПΔ: Count Dracula 174

My Mr Harker has my humble apologies, for his daring has shown me a new side to him, daring to disturb my sleep, but I needed not to wake, for he fled before latent death. Yet, when I offered to throw him to the wolves, he hid behind death. We will miss his humour when he is gone.

C19TΠE: Count Dracula   175

The sindeldi, venturing too close, courteously provided us with a parting feast. But rather discourteously, Mr Harker made a murderous attack on me, and I should have made one on him, speeding my parting guest, for he has now departed before I could say "goodbye". My fly has flown, but cannot get far.

C19PE: Countess Dolingen   85

Not in vain did we watch and wait. The castle proved hazardous, and several sindeldi paid the price for their pluck. I weep not with those who now weep, and they therefore think me weak! Is their weeping strength, as they claim, or weakness, as we have been led to believe? Working with them is enough for me to learn for now, but even that is a valuable lesson. Jumping from the frying pan into the fire, Harker braved a rock climb rather than braving his sealed fate among my sisters. I confess he has earned my respect: inertia twice sealed my tomb! Had Harker guessed that his death and the Count's departure were nigh? I suspect that they have set false trails to bury Harker's true fate. *Ergo*, the Count has intended either to return unquestioned, or at least to be able to return unquestioned. Where Dracula is off to I know not, but saved from the wolves Harker lives bodily, and an undeceased Harker might yet thwart Dracula's plans.

C19TΠZ: Count Dracula   176

My cargo and I took ship at Varna, where I conveyed my thanks to them who conveyed my boxes to the port. For as a parting gift I gave unto them Odin's harvester scythe and a touch of madness, so that each seemed to be—and so died—the mortal enemy of each. A pleasant ending to their loyal service, of which they will speak no more! The sailors of *Demeter* too would not, I am sure, wish to betray my journey, and have so far provided lite snacks in my service. Now we approach our final port of call, Whitby, with captain, first mate, and one hand, showing full sail, and myself at the wind's helm. I shall enjoy a hearty meal before I land.

C19TΠH: Count Dracula   177

Before I was ready to dine, the vile mate tried to stab me, then fed the sharks. But the kindly captain tied himself to the steering wheel with a crucifix, awaiting my pleasure—what fools these mortals be. There

I have left his body, drained and dangling—at half-mast—in courtesy to my erstwhile host who seemed so strangely attached to it.

C19TΠΘ: Count Dracula   178

After my storm the weather is sunny at Whitby. Avoiding Customs, I disembarked as a mad dog. None hindered me save one rash dog—speedily rebuked for its rudeness—and one brash dunamos, suspicious of my plans. Awaiting my boxes, I walk the streets of Whitby. Do I believe in love at first sight? Aye, for today I met my perfect slave. She is a somnambulist, a night-walker even as I am a night-stalker, and of delicious and rare AB+ blood. Moreover, to human eyes she is a young and innocent beauty, which oft makes the best bait. Besides, she is conveniently of London Town: having discarded my brides I urgently seek more eyes and ears. If her resistance proves strong, she will simply die by the wayside, as a flower plucked from its soil. Yes, Miss Lucy Westenra, will you now be mine; may our blood entwine?

C19TΠI: Count Dracula   179

Little Lucy has met me at church, though I prefer the outside to the inside, a church-yard to a church-pulpit. Romans believed that the church was a bloodsucker—*hic sanguis meus est*—but its blood is not my blood, nor is mine its. At variance, it would deliver Lucy from me, whereas I would deliver her from it. But its hope is vain, its master a tyrant. Its minions annoy like buzzing flies on a hot day. One buzzed me away from Little Lucy: it was neither the time nor the place to swat it. Once I settle in in my London digs, away from prying eyes, I shall be free to deal with flies. This fly seems to be a chaperon of Little Lucy: she had best beware of interfering with my lawful prey.

C19PΘ: Countess Dolingen   88

My patient is much improved. I helped him reach Cluj, and shadowed him to the hospital in Buda—where I have been keeping watch. He has recovered to the point of causing a letter to be written to his betrothed. Absent, she is intangible. I am curious: why do humans itch for the intangible? To my mind, it's his nurses and protector he needs. I have lost sight of the Count, but if he needed Harker's death, then he might already be returned from wherever he went, and be on Harker's trail. In extremity I would call for human help, for the Count is increasingly vulnerable to human weapons, and I would almost die to see him die.

C19TP: Count Dracula   180

I am rested up and ready to roll. My boxes leave today for my new home. Little Lucy has been a treat, and I have an open window to her soul and blood. Her cautious chaperone turns out to be a Miss Mina Murray, a close correspondent of Mr Harker. Of what happened to him I have had no word, and would be worried if I had, for my enemies might cross the bridges to my past and find me. He was to have been a distraction during my departure, lest my brides be tempted to follow me: they travel the faster that travel alone. It might be that Little Lucy will hear from Miss Murray if he returns to her— she is soon to return to her London home, where we may more conveniently meet. But by canyon or claw I suspect that Mr Harker has met his maker, in which case his letters should deflect attention away from my whereabouts.

C19TPA: Count Dracula   181

I might have misjudged Mr Renfield, for he has a madness I could not have anticipated. Instead of lying low in the district, he has become lodged in a hospital for the diseased of mind, a description perhaps applying to most of their sad race. Not all are compliant: I have known some resist me by strong will and goodness; he resists by strong will and madness. He says that he is *zoophagic*, and has begged to become like me! The fool thinks that a slave can become a master; a human become a vampire; a Terran become a Simbolinian. He might as easily become a woman! Tonight he drew unwanted attention to me, me who would lie low, and by the ill will of Usen his compound abuts mine.

C19TPB: Count Dracula   182

Another pleasant visit to Little Lucy, now home in Hampstead, a short flight from my home. Her taking the air at Whitby has done us both good. I am enchanted by her weakness of will, and in her case am prepared to overlook her goodness. Do I still love her? Why, yes, as dainty a morsel as ever I grew fat on. Perhaps it will be better to cut her intermediate life short, and not to spin it out, for those she accounts friends—especially a new acquaintance from Amsterdam, a

Mr van Helsing—stick their noses into my affairs. Claiming to be wise, her Mr van Helsing cites the lore and experience of the ancients, even the witless Black-heads. Such simpletons seek our souls' wellbeing by separating us from our bodies! Ignorant apes! They vainly imagine that set free, we Pneumata—whom they think are abnormally blighted Psuchai—become aggeloi, tertiary Powers of the Enemy! Their infuriating mixture of benevolence and brain-dead blundering is droll yet deadly dangerous to us. Their 'setting us free', 'restoring us to humanity', condemns us to eternity, but if they knew that we pre-existed their own kind, they would the happier kill us— xenophobes!

C19ΣΓ: Countess Dolingen93

Harker and his bride have returned to their homeland. I shadow him, hoping he will prove as wounded bait to shark. By supererogation I must exculpate myself from Dracula's defiance to the queen. Though banished, I have used back channel links to deny any foreknowledge of his plans, and unofficially Rangda has permitted me to seek and destroy the Count if I can. She cares not if I die in the process.

C19TPE: Count Dracula   185

My newfound friends have kindly refilled Little Lucy. On the one hand, I am delighted to again drain her, whom they say has been quite gay. On the other hand, it annoys me that they seek to dam what I seek to drain. This is turning into an infernal game, at best a bittersweet diversion, a farce. The serious side is that that man from Amsterdam—what he, an ethnic Jew of the Church:Catholic, calls Mokumalef—is disseminating false information about me and, what is worse, true information. Lest the queen gets on my scent, I must downplay both my identity and my location. Perhaps I should simply leave Little Lucy be, and disappear forever off their radar, but I will be damned if I let little humans chase me away from my lawful prey. A direct attack on my enemies could whip up waves, begin some sympathetic movement, and make me manifest. No, things must die down. Little Lucy must die.

C19TPZ: Count Dracula   186

So, they've turned to garlic! Either they simply identify me as vampire—for some believe that garlic is some magical defence—or they identify me as Dracula—in which case they know me to be alliumphobic. My fears are few, but I fear garlic like the plague, for it triggers great ordeal. I suspect that these simpletons simply know me to be vampire. So, like chess they make their move, but like chess I can counter and they cannot win against a master. This time my victim's mother proved my best friend, removing even the scent of that pestilent weed, letting me without let visit her sweet Little Lucy afresh—as fresh as a rose. Will they never tire of refilling her?

C19TΡΘ: Count Dracula 188

A charming trip to the zoo allowed me a chance to commune with nature. Afterwards, we resumed our little chess game. Their knights failed to protect their queen, and my wolf took the castle, exposing their queen. I hung around to hear their plans. Within a load of poppycock, the good Professor Helsing said that "God sends us men when we want them". Humbug—how he loves to prolong the game. All this to-ing and fro-ing has passed the point of pure exasperation, and now they must concede the game, for it is high time she died unto me.

C19TΡΙ: Count Dracula 189

Snelling, Smollet, *et al*, obligingly distribute my boxes around town. Thus I can rest in peace, without my psychic signature being perceived by my people, and multiply my killing fields. Too much in one place draws too much attention and catches the red eye of Rangda. I am also endangered by the Dawn, and even by my brides whom I have deserted. Still, I have long prepared the soil with properties sufficient to shield me from their telepathy. Friend Renfield remains a fly in the ointment, seeking to stop my freedom of movement so as to keep me to himself. A fly too possessive might have to be swatted.

C19TΣ: Count Dracula 190

I have summoned Little Lucy to me, and she sleeps the sweet sleep of death. See where they have laid her, my beautiful corpse! See, even a lovely gold crucifix—spitefully intended to keep me at bay! I would have happily worn it in token of triumph, had not an ever so honest family maid pipped me to the post, stealing it from under their noses, they who malignantly stuck garlic under mine. Her chrysalis body has my close attention—my nature controls hers until she is developed under my dark wing. Once she has attained her full thelogenic potential, secure as my slave she may reassert her own inherent charm.

C19TΣB: Count Dracula   192

Some miles northeast of the Welsh Harp, in a churchyard she sleeps. Thoughtfully they have selected a suitable tomb for her to freely come and go. Already she seeks out little children; later her powers will grow. Now she but savours; later she shall slay. Boxes placed in Piccadilly allow me easier access to her. But I seek other brides, and extra eyes and ears are for now more important in quantity than in quality. As my power base extends, I can at leisure be choosy, dumping less useful in favour of more useful slaves: too many would be too draining. But I think that Little Lucy might long retain her value.

C19ΣH: Countess Dolingen   97

Shadowing Harker and his wife, I have discovered the whereabouts of Count Dracula. A developing circle of humans has formed, dedicated to the idea of rescue work, of he and any he has bound to this world, that they might see the light and trot off to higher spheres. Pah! Should I ally with the silly secondborn, as I have with the sensible sindeldi? Yet strange though it be, their superstitions are both as harmful enemies and helpful friends to them. Helpful, in having some ideas about killing us; harmful, in that they don't see what we really are, and therefore rely rather on hit and miss remedies. Being vampire, I see yet may not enlighten them, for we must never be more than a fantasy to them. If I exterminate the Count, I will win credit; if I expose our people, I will win censure. I must navigate between the devil and the deep blue sea, if I am ever to reach quiet waters. But can I help them—and they me—by remaining unseen by both them and the Count who spies on them?

C19TΣΔ: Count Dracula   194

Very disturbingly, my enemies befriended my slave: the cage opened; the bird flew. The chrysalis days are so vulnerable, and she even reverted to her old human apprehension in beholding a mere crucifix. Having learnt the art of shapeshifting through cracks, she was baffled by finding them blocked, in blind panic blocking my telepathic control. I could have suggested that she simply removed the seal once they had left—a simple enough expedient—or relocated. I felt her fears and her sorrows. Poor girl, prevented by mere putty! I learnt later that gullible but galling Mr Helsing had believed it to be a magic mix! Hogwash! But poor Little Lucy danced to their tune, deaf within the coffin of her own mind, trapped in or trapped out as the puppet masters chose, dancing with my malevolence but not to my mind. Dread deafened her, and I, I was thwarted by mere garlic, and misjudged their cunning. Staking her heart to cut her link to me, and severing her head to cut her will's link to her body, freeing her forever from mortal life. Well, what Usen will make of her I neither know nor care. I will find others.

C19TΣE: Count Dracula   195

Last night monsterish Mr Morris took a pot-shot at me, as I, as an interested party, did but listen in on their plans. How rude! And Mr Harker—ever a thorn in the flesh—has unearthed my main hideaway, incidentally digging up my connection with Mr Renfield. I am tempted to exterminate the vermin. Mr Helsing understands well our thelodynamic power of morphing, and of control of weather and wolves, but understands little the destiny of the Children. He really does believe that in spite of their innate spiritual orientation, their feet must walk in paths of flame if they die under vampire control, even if doing their duty to Usen—as if Usen is under our feet, unable to keep his own! Would that that was true!

And then he spouted out a load of tosh about suicide soil, grounded on where Little Lucy once sat! His absurdity is simply gorgeous, but all the same I wish the rabble-rouser damned. His rabble turned up at my house, after visiting Dr Seward's. There, they were surprised by Mr Renfield exhibiting words of knowledge—simpletons, my student's simple telepathy needed no miraculous source. Here, they were surprised by my counterattack, but they play the game well and live to fight again another day. They plan to trace me through the psychic dampening boxes, and on finding me at rest—increasingly I need regeneration—to kill me if they can. To stalk their schemes, I have now recruited Mrs Mina Harker, and look forward to hearing the pillow talk of Mr Harker. I shall post-haste place one box portside, in case they box me in and I must depart in haste.

C19TΣZ: Count Dracula   196

The best laid plans! These pernicious people are troublesome to me. Today I crushed the life out of the life-crazed Mr Renfield, as well as destroying their documentation about me. After satiating myself on Mrs Harker, I attempted revenge on her husband for his unwanted interference—death at her lips. The dastards disturbed my pleasure, and almost I forgot myself and tore them limb from limb where they stood—as if their crackpot crucifixes frightened me off as a feebleminded fiend! But I managed to choke back my rage: they know my secret, but their corpses must not alert others at this stage, so I chose flight not fight. I have informed Mrs Harker that I have longterm plans for her—I still hope to dominate her beyond death. Dematerialising nigh exhausted me, but now my Mina's blood restoreth my soul. I wonder what they will be saying of me now— there was too much moonshine in what I last overheard.

C19T: Countess Dolingen 100

I watched as the Count flew away, but had I followed he would have seen me. The headhunters seeking him speak much folly, but still endanger him: why did he not slay them? The poor girl is almost his, and threatened an altruistic suicide—I am impressed by her; she has a good heart that resists the Count. They insist that she lives for now, for they have a theory that a die-as-slave-soul-forever-enslaved, but a die-as-free-soul-forever-free. It is a curious idea, perhaps planted into their hollow heads by Necuratu, since it calls into question the ultimate power and fairness of Usen which their own priests preach: I merely observe. As I watched from the window, a red mark appeared on this girl's head, taken by them as a token that Usen has sealed her unto the day she is to die, a saintly scar of self-sacrifice. They know where the Count's boxes have been stored, and have some plan to 'sterilise' them. Why not simply spill the soil down a drain or into a river? Still, contamination by garlic should do the trick, though the very fact that he knows that they have found his boxes might suffice.

It is funny, but in these last few days when I've seen myself, I seem like someone else. Unimpressed by their brains, I have been impressed by their...goodness. Like my erstwhile lord, I dismissed the two witnesses who braved their lives to speak with him recently, Hamashiachim of the Day. Was it nothing that though strong they turned from the Kingdom of Night unto a minority report? Aeons ago they were as moths around Simboliniad; now as like mere seconds ago, as moths around Hamashiach, whose life we had sought to slay not to serve. Funny enough I feel the stronger for such thoughts, and even daylight seems a wee bit less baleful. I sense no Guardians protecting these mortals, though fortune beyond the common lot is their guardian. Am I being slotted into their fortune? I shall shadow them and see.

C19TΣH: Count Dracula   197

Curse and confound them! I had already decided to leave their fair shores, but they simply could not let me leave in peace. Having checked my other lairs and found them found, I checked my Piccadilly mansion to confirm my travel plans. My enemies were there. Worse, there *she* was, that draggle of a Dolingen, the uninvited guest most unwelcome. Is she playing shadowminder to them? As a rat she sat in a corner, trickling thelodynamic power through human arms—a new trick. Her full strength would have cremated their arms, but neither she nor I can risk public combat. I presume that she merely wished to warn me away, while letting them imagine that their own puny power was flowing through their little crucifixes, herself hidden from them. I painfully yearn to rip her limb from limb in cold revenge. My berth paid in cash, I sail from Doolittle's, leaving my new slave-bride ashore.

C19TA: Countess Dolingen   101

Though the Count wanes while I wax, I do not fancy my chances. I think my best shot remains with the headhunters, for they have at least rudimentary insight, and can easily summon their kind at need—to which end I can protect them. In making the woman his eyes and ears, the Count has overlooked the saying of the sauce being suitable for goose and gander, for she has been used to speak what he sees and hears—a conduit for foe and friend alike. Their leader continues to needlessly frighten the girl, but seems to me to at least speak what he believes, and to mean well. For all the wrong reasons he rightly realises that the Count poses a unique danger for mortal man: some countries that do not fear tigers fear man-eaters, the warped of the tiger world.

The Count's vessel sails to Varna. Were he smart, he would bury his tracks by forcing it to some backwater port after murdering its crew, but he is blithely unaware that his departure has been noted, so why should he not follow his natural course home? He will soon be too far to see or hear his enemies' plans, yet I can increase her telepathic range if needs be, and over seas is far easier than over land. When she is alone, I will put in her mind that she should not see and hear what the Count should not: it is more blessèd for him to give than to receive.

C19TΣI: Count Dracula   199

The pleasantly uneventful voyage was somewhat sullied when I felt Mrs Harker nearby. That could only mean that she is awaiting me at Varna, presumably at their bidding. So, they have traced my departure and must be anticipating my arrival, necessitating that we bypass Varna on my way to the port of Galatz, where I may swim once more in the delightful Danube. The fools must fear letting her run loose, lest they lose her soul which I would not loose. Their absurd notion will be to kill me, then—they will imagine—it would be mercy to kill her! In hope that her presence might reveal their schemes, I enquired as to their plans. Alas, they have shielded themselves from her, so she is in the dark and useless to me until I rescue her. I enquire no more. She shall be sent back to London, once I have snuffed out their lights, and in my own land that is easily done by my wayfarers or by my wolves.

C19TT: Countess Dolingen103

Until today nothing of note has happened since that murder on the Orient Express to Varna, which fortunately did not embroil my company. But unfortunately and unavoidably, today I had to briefly stop shielding Mrs Harker and hide, for one of the sisters flew by. Back in my old hunting grounds I feel hunted, howbeit half-heartedly, for presumably they presume that I, and perhaps the Count, am far away. Left unguarded, Harker's wife was revealed and was probed by the Count's mind—unperceived I tapped in. So far he knows not that van Helsing uses hypnosis to tap into his mind—

happily he underestimates his headhunters. To re-shield her mind from him would now be to reveal my presence, and tempt him to summon his brides. I must allow him to access her mind on demand, so at most he might continue to assume that he needs only to fight the headhunters. Needless to say he will not now land in Varna, for although his box has for now lost some importance, it can enshroud his return and be used to escape again.

C19BT: Count Dracula   200

I forwent grazing on Captain Donelson and his jittery crew. But had they carried out their threat to turf my precious box overboard, I would have drained every last mother's son of them, even had it meant flying home to face the music of Rangda. Their captain held their hands off, and is rewarded by survival. Mr I-for-Immanuel Hildesheim survived also, but for purpose and pleasure, middleman Skinsky went down well. My hunters are simpletons, but not such as cannot figure out that having bypassed their port, I would head to one closer to home. Therefore, cutting out the middleman will fox my foes—if they trace me to port. I now travel within my box, concealing my presence from the Night, and have slowed down my metabolism, deep-sleeping lest any psychic vibration be perceived by the queen's agents. While in or near my box, I should be safe from the queen. Glad will I be to see the end of the Siret and Bistriţa, and to put my feet up at journey's end. There it might be that I can overtly deny my flight, yet covertly plan another. Need Rangda ever know of my playful journey there and back again? I wake next in Transylvania.

C19TZ: Countess Dolingen   106

Arriving at the port of Galatz, the headhunters divided into three, covering the waterways, their banks, and the quickest way to the castle to cut off the Count. I chose to remain with the leader, who took with him Harker's wife, increasingly becoming the Count's slave-wife. Within sight of the castle they sheltered from the snows of the night. I erected an invisible chain around the girl, lest she slay the sleeping professor and join my sisters. Her slavery to their master called unto them, and they sought her out. Had I not been there they would have taken her, but I withstood them. My powers have risen, and they sensed that and fear me the more. They would have been wiser to have risked open combat. Indeed, as if by the cunning of the

Count, at one stage the potty old professor provoked them. Had they yielded to his challenge I might have slain one, perhaps wounded all, but they would have slain me and the humans, who move inexorably towards having their heads. But they were blind to their danger and, content to try tempting van Helsing out beyond my power shield, withdrew with the coming of light. Harker's wife too they tempted, and had she added her will to theirs, she could have broken free from me. They now know that I have returned, but not that the Count is nigh, nor of his plans.

C19TH: Countess Dolingen   107

Things have gone surprisingly well. The professor left Harker's wife sleeping. Though vainly he trusts in the magic circles of his mind, instead of in the sindeldi who were there, guarding her from any wolves. I shadowed him into the castle, where he showed great canniness, and also great resolve. For one by one he killed my sisters in mercy. Naturally they opposed him, but one by one were caught napping, and I was on hand to prevent each one from waking the others. Each one I fettered by brute force, even forcing a smile to surface as each was slain. Totally opposite to the truth, the benign professor believes unquestionably that each desired most what in fact each desired least. His aioniology is based on the false assumption that they were innately human, Psuchai, rather than Pneumata. In both their binding and their loosing, in the eyes of my people I am innocent of their direct deaths—the sealing of their fate, exclusion within the Timeless Void. For a human loosed them whom I had merely bound. Each body, being of the fire clan, rapidly reduced to smoke and dust.

The humans then left, just in time to bar the Count's Roma from the castle road. His lackeys seemed in haste to gain the protection of the castle, fearing perhaps the howling of the wolves which could be heard as the sun set. Others of the headhunters rode up valiantly from north and south. In the swirling snow I too advanced, though none I think divined my flowing form. I saw as soon as the box was opened that the Count had added the precaution of deep-sleep to his silver-soil dampener, so concerned was he of the queen's wrath for breaking his house-arrest. It might have been of some satisfaction to him to have known that she had been unaware of his whereabouts, but his overprecaution was his undoing. His waking power remained far more than mine, but in seeking to remain semi-comatose until secure, he had gravely miscalculated. The triumph within his eyes soon paled into comic despair as he felt my hands of power pinioning his body within its tomb, for there he died, that fell dragon of the fire clan, and his body melted away—to meet his brides, if the romantics speak true. Else not to meet them—if rumours of the Timeless Void speak true, for they speak of only bitter loss within the confines of darkness and despair, where shades know not the bonds of friendship, being self-enslaved.

I, having moved cautiously towards the Light, still hold little hope of any better fate. I have long opposed Usen, and he is not one to forgive or forget. The girl, released from her master's will, proved a happy sight for the sore eyes of their dying warrior, Mr Morris. May my own eyes close, be it in ten hundred thousand millennia more, with the happiness of having tasted of the virtues I have seen within Usen's children. As for happiness beyond, I do not believe in fairly tails.

THE END

Cosmology
Being Types

- **Powers** (Type 2 beings)—spirits created within the Dynamic Bubble: unfallen Powers were Philikoi; fallen Powers were Turannoi. Three ranks/levels: Cosmic—could oversee a planet; Kingdom (unfallen guardians and fallen dunamoi)—spec ops or province based; Channels/Agents—tertiary helpers, foot soldiers, aggeloi (unfallen) and diaboloi (fallen).

- **Pneumata** (Type 3 beings)—cosmic-born spirits, created outside the Dynamic Bubble. Some were as powerful as Kingdom Powers. Disobedience diminished their power.

- **Psuchai** (Type 4 beings)—global-born spirits, such as sindeldi and humans.

The Pantocrator created Powers, Pneumata, and Psuchai, which could fall into disobedience. Powers outside the Dynamic Bubble could not change, but the hidden rebellion or submission of a few—systemic or superficial—could surface in real time. Phusika (Type 5 or lesser beings) he also created through intelligent code, but not in his Image. But to those of mortal souls, he gave images, dreams.

Spirit Kingdom Types

- **Necros**: actively against creator and creation

- **Night**: actively against creator

- **Grey Zone**: betwixt kingdoms, passively towards creator and creation, uncommitted

- **Dawn**: actively towards creator and creation

- **Day**: Hamashiachim actively towards creator and creation

The **Necros** is dark in heart and mind; the **Night** is dark in mind: in general terms, both are of the **Dark**. The **Dawn** is light in heart; the **Day** is light in heart and mind: in general terms, both are of the **Light**. The **Grey**, unsure and unaligned, is unconsciously of the **Light**.

Primary Characters

Agnes: Type 3 (Dark) / Noble

Angruin/Drac-ul-a/Urgiri-nuna/Vlad: Type 3 (Dark) / Noble

Anu: Type 2 (Light) / Royal

Azazel: Type 3 (Dark)

Dolingen: Type 3 (Dark to Light) / Noble

Drac-ul-a/Angruin/Urgiri-nuna/Vlad: Type 3 (Dark) / Noble

Elaran: Type 3 (Dark) / Royal

Enki: Type 2 (Light) / Royal

Enlil: Type 2 (Light) / Royal

Erzsébet: Type 3 (Dark) / Noble

Fafnir: Type 3 (Dark)

Fangli/Lókestámo/Alessandro: Type 3 (Dark to Light) / Lord

Hamashiach (Huion): Type 4 (Light) / Sui Generis

Harker, Jonathan: Type 4

Inanna/Ishtar: Type 3 (Dark to Light)

Kiskilla/Lilith/Rátek: Type 3 (Dark to Light) / Royal

Lacrimal/Carmilla/Millarca: Type 3 (Dark) / Noble

Lilith/Kiskilla/Rátek: Type 3 (Dark to Light) / Royal

Lókestámo/Fangli/Alessandro: Type 3 (Dark to Light) / Lord

Necuratu: Type 2 (Dark) / Dark Leader

Ngushur: Type 4 / Royal

Nindara/Wayanár: Type 3 (Dark) / Royal

Noach: Type 4 / Slave-redeemer

Rangda/Calon Arang: Type 3 (Dark) / Royal

Ránpalan: Type 4 / Royal

Rátek/Lilith/Kiskilla: Type 3 (Dark to Light) / Royal

Shesh-kalla: Type 4

Tauresgal: Type 4 / Royal

Ubaratutu: Type 4 / Royal

Urnúla: Type 2 (Dark) / First dragon-mother

Usen/Pantocrator (Deo): Type 1 / The Light / Cosmic Creator

Utu/Shamash: Type 2 (Light)

Vlad/Angruin/Drac-ul-a/Urgiri-nuna: Type 3 (Dark) / Noble

Wayanár/Nindara: Type 3 (Dark) / Royal

Westenra, Miss Lucy: Type 4

Ziudsudra/Atrahasis/Utnapishtim: Type 2 (Light) / Undercover Guardian

Books by this author

Theology

Israel's Gone Global

Israel's Gone Global traces salvation through the term, Israel. Was the covenant with the people-nation of Yakob-Yisrael, crossed out? How eternal is covenant? To examine that, we examine marriage. Can a covenant partner be truly divorced? Has Yeshua-Yisrael mediated a spiritual covenant with a spiritual Israel? Is evangelism of ethnic Jews needless, a priority, or neither?

No one could have everlasting life but for the cross, but has it always been globally accessible? Might any who die as Atheists, Hindus, or Islamists, make heaven? And is eternal life joyful? Is everlasting life fun?

Tackling the question of people who die in infancy (or as adults who never heard the gospel), we consider whether it is fair if only those who don't die in infancy get a chance of eternal damnation (if infant universalism), or alone get a chance of eternal heaven (if infant damnation). Does predilectionism make best sense of biblical revelation?

Opportunities to enjoy eternal life spring from the new covenant—reasons to rejoice. But what about salvation history before that covenant?

∞

Singing's Gone Global

Singing's Gone Global, briefly explores the background of singing, before and into ancient Israel. It examines the impact songs have on those who sing, and on those who listen, touching on spiritual warfare. It looks at how nonsense songs neither make sense to evangelism, nor to the evangelised, and asks, "Is there a mûmak in the room?"

Oddly some songwriters simply misunderstand prayer. Part two covers the basics of the trinity, focusing on the spirit in order to understand types of prayer (eg request, gratitude, adoration, chat), leading in turn to a better understanding of our heavenly father, our brother, our helper, and ourselves in Christ's likeness.

Next we look at some common problems. Part three focuses on problems such as buddyism, decontextualising, misvisualisation, and unitarianism. Diagnosis can help Christ's 'bride' to recover from suboptimal and unbiblical songs (Eph.5:18-30).

Giving a Problem Avoidance Grade (PAG)—an A+ to Unsatisfactory scale—in part four we examine specific songs. Weapons forged (Part three), the mûmakil can be attacked, seeking to save and be saved.

Subsequently the book concludes by showing how Christmas carols may be tweaked to better serve our weary world, rejoicing that joy to the world has come.

∞

The Word's Gone Global

The Word's Gone Global, examines Bible text (trusted by early Islam) and introduces textual critique. It looks at the Eastern Orthodox Bible and the Latin Vulgate. Did the Reformation improve text and translation? Were Wycliffe, Tyndale, and Martin, helpful?

Why did the New International Version begin, and why does it enrage? Why did complementarians Don Carson and Wayne Grudem, clash? Is marketing hype between formal and functional equivalence, meaningless? Which version or versions should you regularly read?

In English-speaking circles, Broughton wished to burn Bancroft's King James Version, yet many KJV proponents—think Gail Riplinger and Peter Ruckman—wish to burn all alternatives. More heat than light?

Grade Charts cover 30+ English versions on issues such as God's name, God's son's deity, marriage, gender terms, anti-polytheism, and various issues in John's Gospel. No, Tyndale was not 'born again'. No, John was not antisemitic. No, he did not disagree with the other Gospels.

∞

Prayer's Gone Global

Prayer's Gone Global, begins with ancient civilisations and prayer (the Common Level). Then it narrows into Ancient Israel and prayer (the Sinai Level). Then it deepens and widens into Global Israel and prayer (the Christian Level). Deity is revealed as trinity: Sabellians mislead.

Relating to the trinity includes the Holy Spirit. We should of course work with him, but should we worship him, complain to him, chat with him? Above the spirit stands the often forgotten father—oh let Jesusism retire.

Authority is another issue. Are we authorised to decree and declare? Is binding and loosing actually prayer, or is it evangelism? Is it biblical never to command miracles? Do we miss out on the supernatural which Jesus modelled for us, too fearful of strange fire to offer holy fire?

You can freshen up your prayer life—ride the blessed camel, not the gnats. Listen to Saint Anselm pray, and C S Lewis and 'Malcolm' discuss prayer, and be blessed.

∞

Revelation's Gone Global

Revelation's Gone Global, is a telling of John's future, as if by a then contemporary named Sonafets speaking to his church about how John's apocalyptic scroll related to their days, and about what was still future to John.

Encouragement is a big theme. Roman persecution was an unpredictable beast which ferociously lashed out here and there— what church or Christian was safe? But God stood behind the scenes, allowing but limiting their enemy, and messiah walked among the churches, lights to the world.

Victory lay neither with Rome nor demons, but with God, and with the warrior lamb who had been slain. Victory was guaranteed, and would finally be enjoyed.

Exhortation was given to believers, to play their part while on the mortal stage. They were to walk in the light, and not to let the show down by straying.

Angels of power, actively working out God's will, far exceed the puny forces against God and his church. His wrath was not pleasant, but could be redemptive until the new age begins.

C S Lewis' essay, The World's Last Night, is briefly examined to enjoin a calm awareness of the ongoing battle we are in, and the brightness to come when the king returns.

∞

The Father's Gone Global

Focusing from God as father, to the specific person of God the father, The Father's Gone Global looks at the biblical parent/child pattern from Genesis, through Sinai, and into the Church.

Abba as a new covenant word expresses deep filial affection even under deep anguish in our Gethsemane battles. Coming through God's belovèd son, it speaks into the church and into our lives.

Though to many the 'forgotten father', human parents/fathers should 'put on' God the father, and his children should 'put on' his son. We forget him to our cost.

Human applications aside, what is the Eternal Society? Is filial relationship modelled by God the son incarnate? Are we to be always obedient to our father and guided by the spirit?

Eschatologically the father will be supreme, but even now he is the one to whom the son points. Christian life should relate to God our father, God our brother, and God our helper, prioritising the father.

Renewal of the church is vital for our confused world, but renewal which downplays the father falls short of the good news which Christ created and the spirit circulates. May this book play its part.

∞

Salvation Now and Life Beyond

Salvation Now, divides the doctrine of salvation into the four main levels of common humanity, the old covenant, the new covenant, and life beyond.

A big weight is put on the term, Israel, as God's master plan. This too has four levels, meaning a man, a people, a new man, and a new people, respectively.

Various ideas of what Christianity, the new covenant for the new people, is good for, and how we get into it and best enjoy it, are examined, and a faith-based inexclusivism is suggested.

Everlasting life is seen as the ultimate goal of salvation, universal meaningfulness and love beyond all fears and pains.

∞

Revisiting

Revisiting The Challenging Counterfeit

Revisiting The Challenging Counterfeit, is an extended review of Raphael Gasson's 'The Challenging Counterfeit' (1966). Raphael was an ethnic Jew whose spiritual journey included many years as a Christian Spiritualist minister.

Today, when psychic phenomena captures the imagination and the bank accounts of popular media, it is useful to unearth the witness of one who had well worn the T-shirt of a medium with pride, only to bury it in unholy ground as a thing of shame and of sorrow and of wasted time.

Challengingly, his book exposes what true Spiritualism is. He had nothing but high praise for Spiritualists, and deep condemnation for Spiritualism. For he had discovered true Spiritualism to be itself a fake of true Spirituality, a mere Counterfeit that, in deposing death in the mind, enthroned it in the soul.

Counterfeit phenomena covered include apparitions, Rescue Work and haunted houses, materialisation of pets, psychic healing, Lyceums, clairvoyance, and OOBEs—to name but a few. This book surveys his exposé of Spiritualism's offer of fascinating fish bait, false food falling short of real food for the soul. Though it takes issue with

Raphael on a number of points, his core insights are powerful and timely, helping us to avoid—or escape from—a Challenging Counterfeit, and to discover true spiritual currency.

∞

Revisiting The Pilgrim's Progress

Revisiting The Pilgrim's Progress, is a re-dreaming of John Bunyan's most famous dream. An ex-serviceman and ex-jailbird, he found fortune, freedom, and fans worldwide.

This dream journey is substantially Bunyan's from this world, and into that which is to come. It is not a fun story, but it has lots of danger, and joy, and reflection on some big life themes.

Profoundly, sinners who become pilgrims become saints. But that can make life more difficult. One big question is, Is it worth it? One big temptation is, Turn back or turn aside. And if you see others do so, that makes it harder not to. Bunyan was tempted. And he discovered that not deserting, can lead to despair. But he also discovered a key to liberty.

Pre-eminently, it is a story of grace which many follow. Grace begins the journey, helps along the way, and brings the story to a happily ever after. Are all fairy stories based on heaven?

∞

Fantasy

The Simbolinian Files

From Simboliniad, a crystal planet long gone, came the vampire race, the wapierze, thelodynamic shapeshifters seeking blood. Most oppose Usen, King of the Light, so side with the Necros. Seldom do the Guardians intervene. These files, secretly secured from various insider sources, reveal something of what they have done, and will do.

∞

Vampire Redemption

Artificial intelligence, created by superpowers to save man, questions man's worth, and becomes The Beast. Escaping into the wild, many discover a wilderness infested by zombies and diabolical spirits. Who will help? Father Doyle? He's tied up with the mysterious Lilith.

Tariq? He's tied up with Wilma. Can the bigoted old exorcist deliver him from evil?

Radical problems can require radical solutions. But does man really need hobs, elves, and the more ancient of days? In the surrounding shadows, vampires and demons form an alliance, raising the stakes against Whitby and Tyneside. Powerful vampires live shrouded within Whitby, speaking of life beyond this galaxy. Is salvation in the stars? Is Sunniva, the despised woman of Alban, worth dying for? Big questions, needing big answers. Not even Guardian Odin can foretell man's fate and, as silent stars go by, one little town must awake from its dreams.

Though The Beast slumbers purposeless and undisturbed, in the far west a global giant slowly opens its yellow eyes and threatens to smother the earth in fire and ice. There is one chance only.

∞

Vampire Extraction

Bitterly long their imprisoned spirits lay, fast bound to Earth's drowsy decay. To the Simbolinian race, there was no hell on Earth, for Earth was hell, and Usen the cosmic jailer. Was it so surprising that as vampires they stalked Usen's children for blood? Most chose the Kingdom of Night, wary of both the Kingdom of Necros and the Kingdom of Dawn.

As queen of the Night, Lilith's story streams through the summer sands of Sumer, and through the green woods of Sherwood. It flags up both dishonour and joy, and cuts across the paths of Ulrica the Saxon and Robin the Hood, as tyrannies rise and fall in merry England. Bigotry seldom has a good word to say about Usen, nor about mercy. Reluctantly, Lilith examines what it means to show mercy, to show weakness. Wulfgar had enslaved Ulrica: is it mercy to let her burn; should mercy have spared Lona? Could Hamashiach turn daughter into sister? Could Count Dracula be turned from his madness? Has Draven really betrayed his mother? Life has many questions.

Tales picture ideas, letting us walk through the eyes of others to better see ourselves. This story exposes subplots behind common history. How these chronicles came to be written up is, in the spirit confidentiality, not for the public eye. What truth is within you must judge. Discrimination is a gift from Beyond, from which the words still echo: mercy is better than sacrifice. Indeed mercy can be sacrifice. Judge well.

∞

Vampire Count

Vampires were not always earthbound, nor are all evil, but being victims of Usen's Eighth Law, his Children became their fair game. Yet the Night Kingdom was divided: some veered to the Necros; some to the Dawn. Who was wrong; who was right?

Long ago one incited his people to racial violence against elven and human kinds. Ever he strove to be king of the Night, and unto Necuratu the Dark Lord he gave the dragon shape. He made war upon the ancient Middle East, even the Nephilim War. Against him the Light raised flood and division.

At last his own people, paying the price of his rampage, bound him in deep sleep. Yet the millennia seemed meaningless to him: even the rising of Hamashiach hardly disturbed his dreams. At last awoken, he and his brides stalked the hills of Transylvania. Only the fear of Lilith—and after her unforgivable sin, Queen Rangda—chained their bloodlust.

Dracula sought escape and autonomy. By cunning and devious means, he immigrated to London via Whitby. Pursuit followed swiftly, with a shadowminder helping a circle of human headhunters, though they sought the death of all vampires.

∞

Vampire Grail

Wulfgar is a vampire, a thelodynamic creature from another galaxy, now locked into our world by one called the Cosmic Jailer. He hides a tormenting secret from his queen, Lilith, which the Necros use as blackmail. She will only go so far with the Necros against Hamashiach—Wulfgar must go further.

Unknown to the Darkness, to bury Hamashiach is to plant the Light. From the buried seed springs life, and humanity must reimagine itself. Longinus turns to The Way, the nexus of the Seventh Age. His spear goes on a special mission to the island of Briton, where Wulfgar lives again.

Logres is centred on Avalon, but raises up Arthur, a man of mixed race, to carry its flag and to protect against the Saxons. But its main enemy is the Darkness, which ever seeks to extinguish the Light it hates and fears.

Finally, it seems as if the Darkness has won, and the dark ages descend. But does the Light not shine in the Darkness? Must Wulfgar remain in the Night?

∞

Vampire Shadows

Dark vampires, hidden within the ancient empire of Khem, fall out with the king who, stirred up by the Necros, enslaves the Sheep People. But Iahveh, the shepherd-divinity, is stirred up, and stirs up a hidden hero to force a way out.

Apprehensively the two vampire-magicians join the Sheep of Iahveh, on their long and deadly trek in search of a promised land. Can any survive?

Warily they ask deep questions. Is Usen evil, as prejudice says? Is he possibly a good jailer? Are his unusual regulations, meaningful? They risk ending up in death.

Neverendingly the Sheep's sorry story drags out in interminable peregrination. Weary of wandering, most would settle for some green pastures and untroubled waters. But as they well know, that would take a miracle.

[i]   In common with many of their kind, these entries have long used human centuries, so C19 means our Nineteenth Century. To this they added a 24 letter alphabet, which need not be explained in full here, having mainly a specialist interest. I have kept the original and added translation. Since a short illustration may be of some specialist interest, some examples follow: KΓ = 13; TKΓ = 113; BTKΓ = 213 (BT becomes a diphthong for 2 x 100); YTKΓ = 1113; BYBTKΓ = 2,213 (BY becomes a diphthong for 2 x 1,000); Ω = 10,000,000. If you can translate 4,297 into ΔYBTΣH, you will have cracked the code.

Not all vampires kept/keep fact-journals, and some kept/keep wish-journals instead, ie of what they hope will happen. Journals can be kept in various forms, such as psychically written from a distance into the structure of a special stone, or simply written at a desk with ink on parchment, and can be encoded. Only a vampire can usually read what a vampire has written. Suffice to say that I have had some insider help.